A FIELD FULL OF FOLK

A FIELD FULL OF FOLK

A NOVEL

by

IAIN CRICHTON SMITH

LONDON
VICTOR GOLLANCZ LTD
1982

British Library Cataloguing in Publication Data
Smith, Iain Crichton
 A field full of folk.
 I. Title
 823'.914[F]   PR6005.R58
 ISBN 0-575-03110-7 ✓

Photoset in Great Britain by
Rowland Phototypesetting Limited, Bury St Edmunds, Suffolk
and printed by St Edmundsbury Press
Bury St Edmunds, Suffolk

THE REVEREND PETER MURCHISON peered into the mirror and thought, "It is true. I am going to die. My face is thinner than it was a week ago. I feel lighter and more frail. It is not that I'm afraid of dying, it is rather that I've lost my faith. Not only that. But I feel that I've not lived, I do not understand the world." And he was filled as he so often was these days with a deep and bitter melancholy and a sense of obscure injustice, as if fate had in some way played a trick on him. Nor did the Bible help him in any way so that when he climbed into the pulpit it was as if he was climbing a ladder into a high wind, and when he arrived there he found it difficult to speak. What should he, the wounded healer, say to them since he himself did not know what comfort to give? The words of the Bible lay dead before him on the page: they had lost their resonance and their power to move him, it was as if he had become too familiar with them. In fact he had retreated from the Bible and now more and more read the poems which belonged to that Saxon period when endurance was everything and hope was scarce. Thus he would chant the lines from 'The Seafarer' and 'The Battle of Maldon' over and over, having been led to them purely by accident, having found them in a corner of the manse library which he had not hitherto explored. Their world became more real to him than that of the Bible partly because it was a world of ice and snow, of deprivation and loss, of courage in the face of despair, of a sea which stretched towards an iron horizon, of the return of the double-voiced cuckoo from the locked graves of winter, of armour worn without hope, of an infinitely overcast sky.

It seemed to him more and more that his life had been lived on the surface of things, that he was ignorant of the agony and grief which many people suffered, and that when he preached he was not speaking to anyone in particular but only sharpening literary phrases: and this though he was married and had two children now grown up and departed from home. I have lived my life, he thought, in the pleasant places, I haven't suffered enough, I haven't the right to speak.

And now as the crab clawed at him he felt more and more soured as if someone somewhere had prevented him from coming to grips, as Beowulf had done, with the monster of the deeps.

As he looked into the mirror he said to himself, "You have, I would say, another year at most."

Dr Stewart had wanted him to go into hospital but he had said, "No, I have something to do. I can't afford to go to hospital now. Give me some drugs to keep me going."

Stewart had raised his head absently from the table at which he had been writing and had stated simply, "Whatever you like."

Stewart of course was very young and it was with difficulty that the minister had stopped himself from saying, "Why do you keep on doing what you are doing? What are you trying to save them for? If there is no meaning in it all why should you bother?"

But he knew that Stewart had never asked himself such questions, though the time might come, and he had after all decided not to embarrass him. He realised that the doctor was staring at him when he left the surgery, but by that time he was thinking about something else.

"I feel," he thought, "as if I should go on a pilgrimage."

But he knew that that was not possible. After all he had a wife (though his children were away from home—one a lawyer and one an accountant) who had helped him a great deal in his work, was popular with the congregation, and quite a lot younger than him. He himself was fifty-nine, she was forty-five.

But the idea of a pilgrimage haunted him. He imagined an autumn through which he could travel forever among the acorns and the fallen apples, among the trees which were losing their crowns and abdicating, among skies which were clear and pure and simple. He imagined houses nestled in the middle of woods, with red roofs, and men and women sitting outside their doors as in pictures. He imagined a paradise of the fulfilled season. But he knew that he would never go on a pilgrimage, and, even as he thought that, he heard his wife driving across the gravel in her busy red Mini.

She came in rapidly carrying her bag with the messages from the local shop. As usual she was brisk and lively, continually in motion, with stories from the village which she had culled like a bee.

"Morag Bheag was in the shop," she told him. "She bought a big

6

cake. Her son George is home from the army. Did you know that he was in Northern Ireland?"

"No," said the minister, "I imagine the army will make him cut his hair."

Some years ago he had trouble with him at Sunday School but all that was forgotten now. No one wanted to have a son in Ireland.

"And," said his wife, "the saga of Chrissie and her boy friend continues. Everyone is trying to find out where exactly they went to but nobody knows. Did you know that all she took away with her when she left was a transistor radio?"

"Isn't that odd?" the minister thought. She had made that break into the blue leaving behind her her husband and her two little girls and all she had taken with her was a radio. He imagined her playing it in a field outside a city where the smoke flowered into the air. What courage it had taken, what irresponsibility, what, perhaps, love! And yet he liked her husband, John Murray, who was a joiner. There was something deeply symptomatic about the girl disappearing into the south with her radio, something gaunt and brave, like a swallow departing.

Mary took the messages out of her bag and laid them on the table. "I love you," he thought. "We have travelled this world together and I love you. What would I have done without you?"

It astonished him that his wife was so continuously in a good humour as if the furniture of the world sufficed for her and she did not want any more than she already had.

"Apples, oranges, and bread," she was saying to herself as she placed the messages on the table. "Milk. How are you feeling today?"

"Better," he replied, though he wasn't. His wife didn't know that the crab was busily eating him and he hadn't told her. She suspected naturally that there was something wrong but not that it was so serious. She glanced at him quickly and then said, "Would you like to go for a walk?"

"No," he said, "not just now. Perhaps later on."

"I had a look at the gift shop," she said. "There's nothing in it. Not really. I can't imagine who will buy the bits and pieces that they have."

"The tourists, I expect."

"Maybe but there's nothing there. Really. I was also speaking to Annie at the butcher's. She has the Jehovah's Witnesses at her house all the time."

"Good," he said. He had visited her a few times and once he had tried to make sausages for her and the kettle had boiled over while he was looking for the milk. She had told the whole village that he might be good in a pulpit but he couldn't boil a kettle and that was a fact. He smiled briefly and almost with affection.

"How about a cup of coffee," his wife asked him and he said, "That would be fine, Mary."

He only called her Mary when he wished to be close to her, and she smiled again, knowing this. He found her movements so exact and harmonious that he would have been quite happy to sit and watch her. Sometimes at certain times of the month she would flare with sudden lightnings and angers, but these would soon pass and she was herself again.

She poured the coffee into the cups and, as he watched her doing so, he thought again of the transistor set playing in a field by itself, or projecting its bright notes from a cemetery as if it were a small gossipy gravestone.

MRS BERRY BENT down to touch the petals of a rose in her garden, the gate of which was flanked by two stone lions set in the posts. Her blue-veined hands were encased in gloves. She had been alone now since her husband had died but she had not allowed herself to become sad and mournful. She had her own routine which she cultivated assiduously, the garden, her grandchildren, her housework. Sometimes she thought of the days when she had been a nurse in Edinburgh, cycling through the city (because of course she could not afford to buy a car), taking down interminable notes from lecturers. How windy and fresh life had been in those days, how full of promise, and in fact hadn't she had a good innings? She remembered, smiling, the day the Jehovah's Witnesses had come to the door quoting their texts and she had stood there and told them,

"Do you see that hill up there?" The two of them had turned and looked at it.

"Well," she had said, "many people can climb that hill. Some may take one way and some another but they all reach their destination at the end." That had shut them up and she had turned away. She was quite proud of that metaphor.

She also remembered incidents from her early days such as when they had an old woman come into the hospital in Edinburgh and she had wakened up and asked her, "Where am I, dear? Can you tell me where I am?" and she had told her (oh, how mischievous she had been), "You're in heaven, my dear," and the old woman had said, "Well, then, can I get a cup of tea?"

She was slim and fit yet, she had a good few years to live. Her mind was keen and fastened on the world around her. She liked bending down in the early morning and putting the small blocks of coal (much of it stone nowadays) into the bucket. She wasn't frightened of death, not at all. Let whoever was there come and take her any time, she wasn't worried. She would meet Angus, her policeman husband, when the time came for her to do so. In his latter years he had grown very stout and she had made him do physical exercises, certainly not as hard as the ones she had made him do when they were young and she had given him the scythe into his hand and said, "Get that flesh off you and do some work at the same time." He had been much more placid than she ever was but well able to deal with the mischievous boys from the village who stole apples or knocked on windows at night. She raised her head and looked down at the railway line. There was a train passing and Lachlan waving to her again. He did this every morning and had done so to her children and now to her grandchildren. On a fine misty morning it was good to see the train sliding along the rusty rails, while beyond them she could see the cattle grazing in the fields and behind them again the hill.

She heard her two grandchildren racing towards the house. Peter, the younger, had said to her one night, "Granny, why does Rhoda have whiskers?" (This was a lady who worked in one of the local shops.) She had almost died laughing for Rhoda had a slight moustache, right enough. The things they came out with.

Peter stopped and looked at the gnome in the garden among the leaves.

"Has he got a letter today?" he asked. She often put a card in with the gnome and read it seriously to him. "It says," she said, "Peter has to be a good boy and I will visit him at New Year."

"Is that right, granny?" he asked, dancing up and down and looking at her with grave unhaunted eyes.

"That's what Mr Gnome says," she answered. Sometimes she saw in Peter a shadow of what her own husband had been, as he stood there so solidly in the sunlight gazing at her with such an unclouded stare. The girl was older, more private, more poetic, and she was called after her mother. Not her own mother who had died of a heart attack at the age of ninety and whose back had been so upright, she who had gone to the lawyer about the croft and had said to him, "I don't want to see any of your letters which I don't understand anyway. Tell me face to face what you are doing about the croft." And she had stood there in the lawyer's office with her hands resting on the knob of her stick. That was the story which had justified the saying, "Touch the flag and hurt the nation", a precept by which to a great extent she had lived.

Peter said, "Do you want to hear my song, granny?" And so he sang in front of her a verse from 'Old Macdonald had a Farm' while his sister Helen giggled as she listened and she herself heard in the accents of the boy the voice of her own son who had left long ago and was now in Africa. Finally Helen couldn't stand it any longer. "Not like that," she said and she herself began to sing, and Mrs Berry knew perfectly well that they were trying to outdo each other, as her own children had also done, that they were striving for her attention.

"That's very good," she said. "That's very good. Both of you," she added carefully.

A thought suddenly landed on the branch of her mind. It belonged to her school-days. She could see Malcolm Currie standing up in his desk with his red knobbly knees, and the schoolmaster, brisk and fiery, was saying to him, "Say 'is'. The third person singular of the present tense of the verb 'to be'. Say 'is'."

And poor Malcolm had repeated after him "Say 'is'" instead of saying "is" on its own while the other boys and girls sniggered uncontrollably and the teacher had flown into a furious rage so that his cinders fell among them. She could see them all so clearly sitting in their desks in that small school-room, in their pigtails and clean flowery dresses while their schoolbags sat at their sides on the floor. And then they had left the school-room shouting "Say 'is'" and they were running down the white road among the larks and the linnets and the clouds turned over and over in the sky, and the trees, loaded with berries, stood burningly by the side of the road along which later her husband would drive his newly bought car, a banger which they had got for practically nothing. And in what a stately manner they had driven along the road, while he stood upright in the seat, and they had sat behind him, herself and her son and her daughters, all away from home now except for Patricia whose children she was now talking to.

"Does the sun wear pyjamas when he goes to bed?" Peter had once asked her seriously. Of course he does, she had said, of course he does. And she had told them a story about a white horse which they would meet only when they went to sleep and dreamed.

"Only then will you see the white horse," she had told them.

And then for no reason that she could think of she remembered Chrissie who had run away with her radio. What a fool she had been!

What a silly fool! She could have told anyone that Chrissie would come to that, ever since she had first seen her going on the train to Glasgow with that scandalously short skirt she wore. Leaving her husband there, and carrying a radio! What a ridiculous thing to do. The girl must be insane. Why, she wouldn't have left Angus for a million pounds.

"I'll help you," Peter was shouting as he ran after her who was carrying the bucket in her hand.

There was nothing like little children. They kept you alive, there was no doubt about it. She waved to Mr Drummond who was passing and who was an elder of the church, upright as ever but some said . . . Well, what didn't they say? And the minister wasn't looking too well, and that was a fact.

She washed the cup and saucer, and threw the water from the basin in an almost transparent curve over the grass. The food she had put out for the birds had been eaten by the seagulls again. She must break it up into smaller pieces.

The train was turning back now and she could see Peter and Helen shouting excitedly as the driver waved to them. The world was good, it was a fine morning, the haze would soon lift.

DAVID COLLINS SAID, "And an ounce of tobacco, please."

"That's right," said Kate who served in the local tobacco and sweet shop.

The old man thought for a moment that she seemed to be talking to him as if he were a child but decided not to make an issue of it. After all, Kate was always bright and kind which was not invariably the case especially with those girls you got nowadays in supermarkets and who were always sitting clicking their machines, and handed you a long strip of paper when they were finished, all the time staring past you to the next person in the queue.

They reminded him of . . . No, better not think about it.

All those sweets that he could eat but didn't have the money to buy. The black balls, the wine gums, the liquorice all-sorts, above all the liquorice all-sorts. His mouth brimmed with saliva.

Kate was so like her mother, the same black hair, the same red cheeks, but that had been so long ago before she married Andrew Lang, the farmer. Why, at the dances she had been the most lively of the bunch, with her head held high, her slim waist, always throwing her legs into the air, while the moon shone down on the corn which was yellow and ripe. And now she had the rheumatics like everyone else and walked with a stick.

And Kate herself was married to a Catholic, wasn't that right, and the priest had come along and told her that she must raise her children in the Catholic faith. Who would have thought that the priest could be so adamant, considering how good he always was to the old folk, always stopping and giving them lifts. But you never knew anyone till he was put to the test and that was a fact.

He placed the change carefully in his purse and tilted his cap as he always did, as he had always done in the past. Be polite, salute, where necessary: after all, there are degrees in this world, not everyone is equal to everyone else.

He left the shop and stood for a moment looking along the little street. Calum, the butcher, was standing outside his shop in his smock striped in white and blue with blood on it. His large red face turned towards David and he nodded.

"A fine day," he said.

"It is that," said David.

Now there was a man who was making a lot of money, who had started off as a gamekeeper on the big estate. A fine poacher more than likely. But there was always a demand for a good cut of meat, not that the sausages you got nowadays were as good as the ones he had eaten when he was growing up. And then, all those days he had spent as a shepherd before retiring, how long ago was it now? Fourteen years. Was it as long as that? His wife had always complained that there was never enough money to buy all the comforts that they needed. How often they had stood outside the window of a shop gazing in while his wife had sighed and he himself had gritted his teeth but said nothing. There must be no more quarrels, there must be no more. Still there had always been the fine spring days when the lambs had whitened the hills, when there was a green freshness in the air, when the skies were so blue that one could lie on the ground and stare into them forever. He had walked about the land like a man from the Bible with his staff in his hand.

"If the lamb is facing you," his wife had said, "if the first lamb that you see is facing you then it will be good luck for the rest of the year."

In those days it seemed that he was a giant who would never be slowed by old age or anything else. And now his son was in New South Wales in Australia and he had married an Australian woman and when he had been home, which was once only, he had looked at his father's sheep as if they were midgets and at his field as if it were a pocket handkerchief.

He turned away towards his house, hearing again, as he so often did, the words 'Quick March' and seeing again that RSM—what had been his name again? Marshall? No, that had been the sergeant, he would get his name yet—that bull-necked RSM and the square on which they had marched with so many others. Then there was the front, the trenches, the wire, the frozen mud, the leap into the blinding sun, the shrapnel exploding around him, the grey shapes appearing in front of him. The straw German swung like a scarecrow when he jabbed at it.

"Harder, man, harder," shouted RSM Morrison, yes, that was his name. "Harder. What would your dolly think of that?" Oh, he had been a foul-mouthed fellow right enough, that RSM.

And then Mons, that day never to be forgotten. What had they seen? The angels with their kindly faces blessing them, bending downwards out of the sun. Matthews was weeping beside him, the others were standing stockstill in amazement. The angels were winged like the Hosts of God. And then it seemed that the guns hit the angels themselves and blew them out of the sky.

Was that place better than where he was now? Better than this lovely village? The thought eeled among the dark stones of his mind.

He opened the door. The cat, grey and fat, came slowly to meet him, arching itself luxuriously round his legs.

Dammit, he thought, I should have got milk. I knew there was something. I'm getting awfully forgetful. And something will have to be done about that window before the winter comes.

He sat in his chair stretching out his legs. Would Murdo come over? He sometimes wished that he would stay away but when he did stay away he felt lonely and sad.

And then there's another thing, he told himself. My son in Australia isn't getting this house. I'll give it to Elizabeth. She is always visiting me, she is always bringing me scones, she is always tidying the house, she is like a daughter to me. And she's only twenty-one, spending the rest of the time working in the bank since her mother died.

I'll give her the house and by God they'd better like it. He stroked the cat which hummed on his lap.

"We could have done with you in the trenches," he thought, "we could have done with you, old lad."

His sharp shaved grey face relaxed again as he thought of Kate's mother. He had kissed her once behind the privy when they were in school together. He might have married her too if he had had the money. But, no, he had done what was right, money wasn't everything even if some people thought that nowadays. He took his ribbons from the drawer and stared at them again. They reminded him of liquorice. By God, he thought, I could show them something yet. I'm not like those old age pensioners you see on TV on Remembrance Day. What did they know of it? And those poppies streaming down from the roof like rain, what were they trying to prove with them? Once again he heard the pipes playing, saw the RSM with his big red face, a cockerel on a dung hill. And heard a knock at the door. Would that be Murdo or Elizabeth? And Kate's mother faded away from the cornfields of his imagination and waved to him as she went out the door, the stick in her hand pointed at him like a rifle.

4

ANNIE, WHO WAS eighty years old but still alert, stood in front of the man from the Jehovah's Witnesses, dressed in her long khaki-coloured coat which she wore at all times. She said,

"I should like you to tell me what is meant by the following passage from Revelations. I shall read it to you.

"'There in heaven stood a throne and on the throne sat one whose appearance was like the gleam of jasper and cornelian: and round the throne were twenty-four other thrones and on them sat twenty-four elders robed in white and wearing crowns of gold. From the throne went out flashes of lightning and peals of thunder. Burning before the throne were seven flaming torches, the seven spirits of God, and in front of it stretched what seemed a sea of glass like a sheet of ice.

"'In the centre round the throne itself were four living creatures covered with eyes, in front and behind. The first creature was like a lion, the second like an ox, the third had a human face, the fourth was like an eagle in flight.'

"Now," she said, "tell me about that."

"Well," said Mr Wilson, peering at her earnestly through his pebbly glasses, "we are told that the Book of Revelations is the most difficult book in the Bible. We are told that this book is called the Apocalypse, which means 'an unveiling'."

"I know that," said Annie. "What do you think I am? You are not talking to an ignorant child, you know. What I want you to tell me, first of all, is the meaning of jasper and cornelian." She stared penetratingly at Mr Wilson who took off his glasses and wiped them with a red handkerchief which had white spots on it. For some reason Annie thought of her long-dead husband and the day he had bought her the ring which she was now wearing on her finger. It had been in Glasgow he had bought her the ring after she had spent an hour or so searching through the shop. Norman had worked on the railway and she had always despised his mentality. "No brain," she would say to the other villagers, "absolutely no brain. How he can understand the signals is a mystery to me." Her husband had been an extraordinarily quiet man who used to leave home and sit in other people's houses for hours in a sort of stunned silence as if he were seeking refuge there.

"Tell me," she would say to the villagers, "if Norman had been alive during the time of the Christians would they have crucified him? He has done more to deserve crucifixion than Jesus did. And so has everyone in this village."

"Jasper and cornelian," she asked Mr Wilson again. "Do you know what they look like? Could you please tell me what they look like."

"Well," said Mr Wilson slowly, "as I was saying they are kinds of precious stones."

"I know that they are kinds of precious stones," said Annie contemptuously, at the same time watching through the window a rabbit racing around the grass. She thought, "If I had a gun I would shoot him and have him for my tea. Rabbits are pests, though I don't believe in myxomatosis. The children like rabbits, they will run after them for hours, spoiling my good grass." Mr Wilson had deceived her, she could see that clearly now. She could see that he was a petty ignorant man with a very low-class handkerchief. He didn't have the faintest idea what cornelian was. He was a fake, she would be better with Buddhism. The idea had come to her recently when he had considered trying to get in touch with Norman who was probably holding up a red flag on a celestial platform in some insignificant corner of hell. "And another thing," she persisted, "what about the twenty-four elders? I shall have to speak to Mr Murchison about it. I'm sure he doesn't know. Why doesn't he have twenty-four elders in his church? It says twenty-four elders clearly in Revelations. There is such a lot of ignorance about it all." She thought that Mr Wilson probably had a wife who wore pebbly glasses, and innumerable pebbly-glassed children as well.

"And what," she asked him, "is the meaning of the lion and the ox? Is the ox connected with the Nativity and the stable?"

Mr Wilson said, "We know that the Jews divided the world into this Present Age which is bad and the Age to Come which is good." His stomach rumbled and he felt embarrassed: his wife had told him that his breath was rotten.

"The Beast in Revelation," he continued, "stands for the worship of Caesar." She looked at him with blazing contemptuous eyes. What a strange woman she was! How had she managed to retain her questioning nature for so long and why did she always wear a khaki coat? What submerged army did she belong to? Perhaps she was some kind of a witch?

"I think that will be enough," said Annie. "It's clear that you don't know any of the answers to my questions. You won't need to come any more." She talked to him as if she were a teacher dismissing a dim-witted pupil. "I shall have to turn to the East after all," she said. Mr Wilson had an uncharacteristic thought. Why, he asked himself, doesn't this woman drop dead? It was such a terrifying thought that his face paled, and anguished sweat beaded his brow. What is happening to me, he thought, that was an awful thing to think of. On the other hand she showed such ingratitude, and her contempt was so obvious. I am trying to do my best, he defended himself, I really am. But how can anyone answer the questions she asks? No one had ever asked him before about jasper and cornelian, such questions were not in his opinion theological ones, they were concerned with matters of fact which could be learned at a jeweller's.

He rose, brief-case in hand, which he was sure was shaking. There was a photograph of a man on the mantelpiece and it showed a face which was cowed and intimidated, capable only of a fixed smile which was like a grimace of pain. It was as if the man had been staring at Annie while the photograph was being taken, like a rabbit at a dancing stoat.

"Only from the East will I learn anything," said Annie expansively. How did she have the knowledge that she had an endless time to live? Mr Wilson often felt that he himself didn't have very long to live, what with three children and his wife and the mortgage on the house. And, another thing, he never sang in the bathroom as he had used to. When was the last time that he had shouted out Halleluiah? He had failed again. How did he know that he had failed and this woman didn't know that she had failed? It was a frightening enigma. Whenever he looked at her he had to drop his eyes immediately: he walked about the world with his eyes turned earthward. He belonged to the meek, and that was true. But this woman had an almost dictatorial self-confidence.

19

"I'm sorry," he said in a low voice, feeling like a dismissed servant who has worked out his notice.

"From the East," said Annie triumphantly. What a strange little worm this man was with his winding snaky blue tie and his blue collar and his look of an insurance man! How could such a man, such a dwarf, bring her news of the triumphs of Revelations, tell her about jasper and cornelian, the lion and the ox? She had always known that this village was not her true place, that it was not in her fixed stars to be trudging about with a message bag, that the measure of her worth was the heavenly arcade of jewellery and tawny lions. How had she put up with Norman for so many years? And as for the minister he was clearly a fake as well. Where had he come from anyway? Was it Edinburgh? No, she was sure it wasn't Edinburgh, it was probably Lanark. No, there was something small about him, too. She needed worlds to stretch herself in, to yawn like a lioness.

"You may go," she told Mr Wilson. She watched him walk down the pathway and enter his old car which banged and spluttered and then turned a corner so that she could no longer see it.

"Silly little man," she thought, as if she were engraving the words on a gravestone. Last time she had been at Norman's grave she had seen a worm winding its way along like a tiny little train. She had ground her heel into it and turned and turned it. "Little bastard," she thought. "The East is the answer. That is where the sun rises."

5

"I think," said Murdo to himself, "that I shall go over and see David Collins, though all he does is talk, about the Great War. It is true that I didn't go to the war because of my glass eye, but I served my country just the same." Nevertheless, had being a postman been as glamorous as fighting at Mons or Loos? True, he had been a very good postman, making sure that his badges and boots were highly polished just as if he had in fact been in the army. Only the other day he had seen a postman in sandals and football jersey, and if he hadn't been carrying a mailbag he would never have known he was a postman at all. Things had changed in the service right enough. When he had been a postman he would only give the letter or parcel to the addressee and under no circumstances to anyone else. He would go down to the field where the addressee might be scything rather than give the letter to his wife or mother or brother or sister. He blinked with his one eye in the autumn sun. Maybe he should have got married but he never had, and that was that. Latterly on his rounds he had seen many strange things. Why, in the village of Westdale he had seen in the early mornings strange cars parked outside certain houses, though he would never tell anyone. And then there had been the time when Mrs Glass, who was no better than she should be, had taken a parcel from him, wearing practically next to nothing. How he had blushed and stammered while she had looked at him in an amazed manner as if he were a species from another planet!

Quite apart from his work as a postman he was an elder in the church because he had more time to do the work than many of the married men, and as well as that, again because of his wifeless state, he was always winning prizes for his garden. His only rival in that was Mrs Berry, who, like himself, spent a lot of time trimming the roses and planting new seeds. But this year he had won the cup again and perhaps he would keep on winning it till he was planted under the flowers. There was nothing in the world like seeing a flower growing to its full colouring and shape in the height of summer. It was like nursing a child through all the tribulations of life. Now, David Collins couldn't do that, all he could talk about was death and battles, and perhaps he hadn't done as well in the Army as he said he had done. Anyone would think that he had won the First World War by himself. He was always going on about that wound in his leg. Why, he hadn't walked or marched as much as he himself had done on those enchanted mornings when the summer returned and the world was wreathed in a heat haze, and you could watch the ducks in the water, and the trees were putting on their berries and there was a stillness everywhere so that you could see the green leaves perfectly reflected in the lochs. There had been nothing like bringing letters from all the corners of the earth to old ladies staying in scattered cottages all over the village. And then there were all the catalogues they would send for, the divorce papers, the bank statements. He recognised them all though of course he would never open a letter.

Still there was no doubt about it, David Collins was growing quite odd. One day, he, Murdo, had said to him, "How are you today, David?" And David had turned a bristling face on him and had said, "It's none of your business how I am. You keep your questions to yourself."

It was almost as if David thought he was spying on him. But that had passed and David was quite normal again, apart from taking out old khaki shirts and washing them and hanging them on the line, and as for that woman Annie she was even queerer with her religions and her farmer's wellingtons. Mrs Berry was all right but then she had her grandchildren to keep her company.

Now there was another thing that had happened recently. That girl Chrissie had run away from her husband and had only taken her radio with her. It was a poser right enough. Imagine that, leaving her children behind her and taking her radio. And her husband was earning good money, too, as a joiner. She had just jumped on the train when he was at his work and that was the last anyone had heard of her. It was said that she had gone to Glasgow with that fellow who had sometimes visited her husband during the tourist season. It was funny, that whole business. He wondered what his mother would have thought of it, she with whom he had stayed till she had died at the age of eighty-seven, almost blind but still powerful in her will. If it had not been for his mother he would have married. He remembered how he had used to leave her in her bed while he would go down and scythe the corn in the field next to Mrs Berry's and he would feel stirring within himself the sap of life—O the shameful sap of life—while he wished that his mother would . . . No, he had better not think of that. And then there had been the day of the gale when he had seen his cornstacks shake in the wind and he had thought, "Go on, lift yourselves from the ground, clear off to Alaska, take your big strawy bums from here." But they had after all not moved and the clouds had raced across the sky and in the morning uprooted trees had blocked the road but his cornstacks were still there. That had been the year one of the church windows had blown in, the one with the picture of Christ on it as a yellow shepherd, among a flock of sheep. The minister had really looked shocked that day.

"It's odd, isn't it?" he had said. "Isn't it odd that the window of the house of God should have been shattered?" A pale, thinking man, the minister, not like the one before him who had been hail-fellow-well-met with everybody and with his red healthy face might have been a farmer. Still, the thing was to keep the house tidy and not drink. Drink was one's downfall, no question of that. He had a good idea that David Collins drank though he couldn't prove it. One morning he would have to look in his dustbin to see if there were any empty bottles.

He prepared to go over and see David. Together they would watch the TV, though it was only a black and white one, and then he would come home and make himself a cup of tea and go to bed. And then there was the meeting about the church hall on Friday. Now, if it was up to him the young people wouldn't get it for a dance.

6

Now more and more the Reverend Peter Murchison felt disturbances within himself as if there was some volcanic evil that was trying to get out, a demon that possessed him like the demons mentioned in the Bible. When his wife was out visiting the sick and the bed-ridden he thought that perhaps she was betraying him with another man: and yet how could that be? He felt as if he wished to punish her, to cut her out of his meagre will, to leave to someone else, as a final unforgiving insult, whatever money he had. "I am sure she is betraying me," he told himself. "What about that David Collins and that Murdo Macfarlane she is always visiting? There is more to this than meets the eye." But he never spoke to her about his suspicions and listened patiently to the stories she brought back from her daily rounds.

One morning he set off for a walk. The hills all around were covered with gorse, the sky was blue, the cows cropped the grass, and now and again he would see a rabbit race across the dew, stop and gaze around it with trembling body, and then resume its running. He didn't know where he was going but found himself outside the house of John Murray the joiner whose wife had left him. When he entered, Murray was sitting at the table with his two little daughters and he immediately got to his feet when he saw the minister.

"Don't bother," said the Reverend Murchison, "don't bother. I'll wait till you're finished." The two girls gazed at him with large round eyes while he sat there and thought, "I have nothing to say to them, I bring no help." He thought that Murray looked much paler than he remembered him and while he was sitting there he was reminded of a cobbler whom he had met in his youth. He too had lost his wife and he used to sit outside his house, repairing shoes, nails in his mouth like thorns, and saying from red distended cheeks,

"Milton, now, did you know that his coffin was five feet eight inches long?" And later,

"Rameses the Second, now, he was an Egyptian, you know. That was what he was, an Egyptian. These are the pyramids I am talking of, you understand." He always seemed to be talking about items he had read in the Reader's Digest. Perhaps that was why his wife had left him, or perhaps it was after she had left him that he began to read the Reader's Digest.

After the two little girls had had their breakfast their father sent them out to play and then turned to the minister with a face of stone.

"I'm sorry," said Peter awkwardly, because he could not think of anything else to say, "I'm very sorry."

"She just took the radio," said Murray stonily, "and she left her two little daughters. And yet the man was a friend of mine. I met him in Glasgow and he used to come here for a few days' holiday now and again. And all the time while I was at my work he was driving up from Glasgow and visiting her. His car was parked outside the door and no one told me."

The minister remembered Murray repairing the roof of the manse not so many months before and how he had heard him whistling above him, as carefree as the birds themselves.

"There's a bit of wood rot, there," he had told the minister, who was feeling sudden twinges of pain which he suppressed, his face twisting. Didn't the Bible warn us that women were not to be trusted, that when you had thought you had them they were far away from you?

"She went away in the red boots I gave her," said the joiner. "Isn't that funny? And yet I was always kind to her. I suppose I'm slow by nature but I was always kind to her. But she was always saying how bored she was, just the same." The minister's eyes wandered across to the sink which was full of dishes, to the frosty shirt hanging over the back of a chair, to the stained cooker which was losing its icy whiteness.

What would he himself do if Mary left him? Would he be able to cope?

"What was there about him that was so special?" said the joiner. Did the man used to have a moustache? The minister couldn't remember, perhaps his wife would.

"I don't know," he answered. There was nothing he could do here. He didn't have that instinctive rightness of response that his wife had, his mind was too reflective. But what could anyone say?

"I don't know," he admitted. "I really don't know." Surely from the distance of imminent death he could speak freely, but the habits and constraints of a lifetime were difficult to change.

"She was always watching the TV," said the joiner helplessly, "and listening to the radio. I used to say to her that she would get square eyes but it didn't matter what I said. That was her life. Perhaps if she had a job, but she didn't want one. I failed her. Where did I fail her?"

"You didn't fail her," said the minister angrily. "You did what you could."

"But she did love me when she married," said the joiner. "I am sure of that. In those days we used to go to the dances but after that we had the children and we couldn't go. She never gave me a sign that she was going to leave. And I never knew that he was visiting her." His huge red raw hands lay helplessly on his knees, and the minister thought, "Here is a man who can make a chair or a table or a wardrobe and he does not know what is happening to him. Is the world run by the devil then? Is he joking with us?" And the devil appeared in his mind, inscrutable and suave as a travelling salesman.

He rose from his chair and said, "I just wanted to see how you were. That was why I came. If you need any help . . ." And his voice trailed away but Murray had ceased to listen to him.

"I'm very sorry," said the minister again. In the old days he would have prayed aloud for the two of them but he didn't feel like praying today.

The two little girls were playing outside the door when he left, taking the path along the stream. Here he stood and watched two small boys fishing patiently for trout and bending down in the slant rays of the sun. That must be the . . . No, one of them was Flora's son, Alisdair, and the other was Hugh, the butcher's son. In the blaze of sun they were netted as if they themselves were the trout. Their voices echoed towards him like chimes from his own youth, We twa hae paiddlt i' the burn, he thought radiantly and regretfully, frae morning sun til dine. Now and again as he watched them they would plunge their hands into the stream and raise them again empty. How can I not feel, he asked himself, how can I not feel anything? The rowan trees are behind them with their red berries and yet I cannot feel anything. I see the two of them only as the repetitions of their parents as if the world were being typed out on carbon paper by a God who wielded the machine with effortless ease. Their voices echoed back to him for they were completely lost in their own concerns. He did not wish to disturb them, they appeared so innocent. And then, as he watched them, they began suddenly to fight about some obscure business of their own. They threw water in each other's faces which were suddenly swollen with rage and then as quickly as they had flared up they calmed down again and were fishing quietly in the stream once more. He raised his eyes to the hill above them whose sides were indented with the dry beds of streams. He was like a lost psalmist whose body was feeling the thorns. Then he saw one of the boys, Alisdair, holding up a small fish which glittered in the sun and the two of them were rushing away from the stream, their little legs flashing past the rowan trees which glowed in the autumn day. It was as if part of himself followed them but not with feeling, rather with conscious regret.

"I cannot go on like this," he thought, "I cannot. How can I live this lie? What should I have said to Murray the joiner? Should I not have wept with him rather than spoken. What Murray required was companionship, his grief to be shared by others."

The minister looked down at his feet where a small plump snail with tiny black aerials had come to a halt in the sun. What is your purpose, he asked it. What are you doing here? Would the world be any different if you did not exist? What for that matter difference would it make if either little Hugh or Alisdair did not exist? The stream was an intricacy of sun and it blazed and flashed at him like a loom, and the hill above it cast a perfect replica of itself into the water like a transparency which had once been imprinted on his wrist.

He walked on. Mrs Berry was as usual working in her garden, bent over her flowers.

"It's a fine day," he said, raising his hat.

"It is that," she replied. Now there was a woman he admired. She had lost her husband, she lived alone, and yet she showed absolute firmness in the face of eternity.

"Coal is expensive now," he remarked, looking at the pile of fuel she had outside the house.

"That's right," she said. There were mounds of sticks lying beside the coal as if she expected to live forever, and yet she must be seventy-six at least. What was the secret of her purposes?

"Won't the minister come in for a cup of tea?" she asked, and without realising what he was doing he had accepted. Her kitchen was neat and clean, the cups and saucers and plates were in their positions, the walls had been freshly painted a lime green.

All the time she was boiling the water she was speaking. "I see the minister was visiting John Murray."

"Yes," he said, carefully removing his hat and laying it on the table.

"It's a shame, that's what it is. That girl has no right to leave her children like that. What is the world coming to? In my young days that would never have happened. She should have her bottom skelped and that's a fact. Going away like that in full view of everybody. It's a scandal."

Her strength invigorated him and he said, "Do you think there is anything to be said on her side?"

"On her side? Of course there is nothing to be said on her side. She's a spoilt brat and that's all there is to it. When she was growing up she was exactly the same. She was a friend of my own daughter and she was getting far too much pocket money when she was a girl. The two of them were at Guides' Camp together and she had a pound a week pocket money. I used to make my daughter cut the bracken and she gave me all the money she earned. It's a disgrace. When I was growing up do you think I had any pocket money? Stuff and nonsense."

Of course she was right. But then how did she know all this, how could she remember it all? We have our certificates, he thought, but someone like Mrs Berry would make a better minister than me. He realised that Mrs Berry lived in the details of the day, that he himself had made an abstraction of the world, that he was not deeply interested in its routine. That had been his mistake. He had been looking for a continual radiance that wasn't there. One should feed on the world as it was. Mrs Berry continued, while pouring the hot water into the tea pot,

"And I know for a fact that he bought her a pair of red boots before she left. Imagine that! And he doesn't make all that money as a joiner. The bin men were telling me all about it. You should see the bottles that were in their bins, they told me. All her drinking. And what do you think Murdo Macfarlane said to me, you know, Murdo. He said, 'She'll regret it, you mark my words, Mrs Berry, she'll regret it. Nothing good will come of it. She'll get no luck from it.'"

"And how is Murdo?"

"Murdo is fine. There's nothing wrong with Murdo. We never had a postman like him. They go about on their bicycles now and in their vans but Murdo walked every mile. Murdo was conscientious. I was looking at him and he keeps himself tidy. He shaves every day, I can see that, and his shoes are polished. There's nothing wrong with Murdo. If it hadn't been for that old mother of his he would have been married years ago. Back of my hand to the likes of her."

She poured the tea into his cup. "Now, tell me if this is too strong."

"It's fine," he said. He felt empty as if he didn't wish to speak and yet when he was young he had never felt like that. Why, when he had been in the theology class, the world had been a sparkle of language. Now it was as if he had lost the ability to communicate.

"And another thing," said Mrs Berry, her eyes alight with intelligence, "she'll find, that same girl, that he'll leave her. I've seen it happen before and it will happen again. As the saying goes, what she put in her head she put in her feet and she'll be sorry for it."

To have such a firmness, such a compass for right and wrong! He gazed at her in amazement.

"But that's the way it is nowadays," she said. "From the cradle they turn on you. They are so impudent that they must be being prepared for a different world. They're all the same, impudent and fearless. All those hippies or whatever you call them. Rubbish and nonsense."

And as he drank his tea he felt an inner peace for the first time for many days. If life were as simple as this!

He made an effort and said, "I heard that Murray used to work late and that she was lonely . . ."

"Lonely," she shouted. "Wasn't he working for her? I've seen the day when the fishermen were nights away from home, and my own Angus wasn't home every night. When I used to live in the islands they told me of a boat that never came home for five nights and when the women opened the door to their husbands on the sixth night they came out of the darkness like ghosts. They were standing one behind the other and they looked like ghosts. I'm alone as she was. So is Murdo Macfarlane and David Collins, and even Annie. We're all lonely. But there's right and there's wrong and she was lucky to have a good husband. She had no call to leave, and imagine these poor little girls have no one but a father to look after them. No, the back of my hand to the likes of that. She was spoilt and that's it. Going off on a train like that to another man."

"And how is Annie?" the minister asked.

"Oh, Annie's all right. There's nothing wrong with Annie. Annie's lonely but she doesn't make a fuss about it."

Suddenly she said, "I remember when I was working in a geriatric ward in Edinburgh we had this old woman and she believed that her husband was going to come and fetch her. Every morning I had to do her hair and prettify her face and then she would wait for her husband. But her husband was dead and she didn't know it. She lived in a world of her own, you understand. The things you see in this world, but I don't have to tell the minister that." She paused and then went on, "Sometimes I used to think that it was the ones who lived in a world of their own who were the happiest. But that's not right. We shouldn't live in a world of our own. When my patients died they used to look at something beyond them, I'm convinced of that. There was a light there that they saw. They were seeing things that we can't see. And there was this old schoolteacher. She would talk about the school register all the time. She thought I was one of her scholars. Of course I was only eighteen years old then. Would the minister like more tea?"

"No, thanks. I'd better be going." What did she really think of him? Her shrewd eyes were examining him and he felt that she saw that there was something wrong with him. Perhaps she did know of the crab that was eating into him and was too polite to say anything. Why for that matter did he not tell his wife? Was it because illness of any kind was a mark of failure, a stigma of dishonour? Was that why he had lost his faith, because he had become ill? Or had he become ill because he had lost his faith? He thought of the time that the two drunken brothers had come to him at midnight to ask him to bury their mother.

"We don't go to church," they had said. "But we want you to bury her. We're strangers here."

And they had even been drunk at the funeral!

"Get out of here," he had shouted at them. "You are desecrating the place." And they had become meek as lambs, his rage was so awesome. And then years afterwards one of them had come back with flowers in his hands and asked him if he could tell him where his mother was buried: he had spent all morning trying to find her gravestone though once he had been there, though drunk. The world was full of strange people and things. Only the other day he had been reading in a newspaper of a blank record that you could buy in order to put it in a juke box in a cafe so that you could have some moments of silence. Buying silence! Surely the earth we inhabited was trembling with madness and derangement. What about for instance that man who kept a lion in his garden?

She watched him as he left and later he was accosted by Annie who had come out of the house in her long trailing khaki coat, stick in hand, as if she were setting off to shepherd the sheep.

"Good morning, minister," said Annie briskly and then, as if she were continuing a conversation which had only briefly been inter-rupted, "I meant to ask you, what is the meaning of the twenty-four elders in Revelations?"

"The twenty-four elders in Revelations?" said the minister blankly.

"Yes, it mentions twenty-four elders," said Annie. "I've read that book through and through. And what's that child doing bicycling along the middle of the road? Hey, you," she shouted, "get off that road and on to the pavement. Yes, twenty-four elders," she con-tinued imperturbably, "why is it that we don't have twenty-four elders? I should like to know that."

"We have the number we have," said the minister, "because that is all we need."

"I am growing disappointed with your church," said Annie. "I think I will turn towards the East. The Eastern religions are more interested in the spirit. Have you heard about Nirvana?"

"I have heard about it," said the minister carefully.

"Well, if you have heard of it you will know that it is a condition of peace. Utter peace, that's what we want. In the Eastern church you do spiritual exercises. In fact it cannot be called a church at all. You have too many women interfering in your church. Why is it Mrs Macrae who does the flowers most weeks? I have enough flowers in my garden."

"But," said the minister helplessly, "you don't often come to church."

"That has nothing to do with it, nothing at all to do with it. Does your wife feed you properly? You look ill. Are you sure you are all right? In the Eastern churches they are not interested in food. Starve yourself and you will see visions. Some of the saints did that. I would say that the saints are very close to the Eastern church. John the Baptist lived on milk and honey. And locusts. And there was a saint who lived on top of a pole for many years. I hear that Morag Bheag's son is in Ireland. That is an example of your Christian church for you. Nothing but guns and mines. And tell me why is the Pope coming there in an aeroplane? They say he's a Communist."

"He's not exactly a Communist," said the minister patiently.

"Well, he comes from a Communist country. He is probably a spy. Have you noticed that he has to be guarded by 'planes in order to take peace to Ireland? That shows you what's wrong." She raised her stick to salute Mrs Berry who had reappeared in the garden wearing leather gloves. "And another thing that puzzles me is why Judas wasn't stopped from betraying Christ. Did Christ know about it and if He did why did He allow him to betray Him? I know that he was hanged just as Christ was and our own St Andrew was hanged on a different kind of cross. But that was an example of modesty on his part. I don't understand why Judas wasn't struck down." She gazed at him sternly and he thought, "How can I give her the long explanation which wouldn't satisfy her anyway."

He thought of Judas sitting by himself in a ditch watching thirty moons shrinking across the Eastern horizon, each of them a silver coin. Then in the dark night of the soul he had climbed the tree and hanged himself. How beautiful this day was, he mused, and yet he felt nothing. How is it that the days pass and they are to me pictures which I myself create, except that now and again some of the pictures snap back at me like a dog at a postman: and one of those recalcitrant pictures is this very Annie who is standing foursquare in front of me at this very moment.

Annie, taking his silence for ignorance, triumphed by saying, "It is from the East that our salvation will come. And, another thing, it says in the Bible that the last battle will be fought there. Is that why the Russians have invaded Afghanistan? That is what I would like to know. The Bible talks a great deal about fire. Is that the atomic bomb? Even the weather has turned against us these days."

Is this another of our disguises and protections, thought the minister, these futile speculations? Do people still believe in horoscopes, in the unchanging influence of the stars, in the fatal luminosity of the sky? And yet certainly Annie showed energy of a kind, which was more than he did.

"I will see you later about this," she said, royally waving her stick and leaving him standing there. Was she occupying herself with religion as a game? Something that would pass the time for her? In her day she had been a clever woman, well able to take a leading part in the little organisations that the village had. Now she had retreated into her superficial speculations about the more extravagant aspects of religion. We set up cages all around us, he thought. If only he could be open again to the world, and bleed. Perhaps he should go and see Morag Bheag: she would be worried about her son who was now in Ireland, and who at one time attended, loutish and ignorant, his own Sunday class.

A seagull alighted beside him on a fence and stared around it with stony eye. Where do you come from, asked the minister silently. All you are concerned with is what food you will get, nothing else. Why were you created, what is your place in the blindingly intricate system? Its breast was snowy white and it had a little red spot on its beak. In the winter months he and his wife would put out bread for the small birds but it was always the seagulls who arrived first, recoiling from the throwing hand, advancing later with large beatings of wings. And how did they always know the bread was there as if they smelt it from vast distances? At the very moment that he and his wife threw the bread they seemed to be there, big yellow-clawed angels of the day, with blank eyes, machines dedicated to greed.

He turned away and made his way home. Curious how that ache for other places had faded now, that desire for voyaging had gone. He was not like those Christians who took staffs in hand and set off into the blue among the bristly autumn, towards the burning city.

33

No, he was here, and here he would remain. But nevertheless he felt unfinished and fragmentary in this marvellous weather whose blueness and calm seemed to last forever. Day after day with no rain, day after day so cloudless and so blue, day after day with the fruit ripening, the roses bowed on their stems, each day a repetition of the previous one, like an image in a mirror.

If only I could feel, he thought, if only I could feel the fruit burst with its sweetness, leaving the husk and the skin behind. But let there be that rich gushing first.

7

DAVID COLLINS BROODED angrily about the two Germans whom he had met in the Post Office. Oh, they couldn't fool him. He knew German when he heard it. He knew that it wasn't French or Dutch that was being spoken. They had the blond hair of Germans too, you could tell them miles away. These damned tourists coming to the village every year, he ought to send them back to where they came from. They looked so innocent too, so young, but he knew what they were really like. Buying stamps in his country, in his village! He had a good mind to make a scene, but in fact he didn't. Perhaps he was getting too old. Maybe if there was a meeting of the village committee he would bring it up. It was far more important than sewage or lavatories. Why, if they didn't watch out they would have Germans swarming all over the villages like midges in July.

He stood in front of the mirror, with his helmet on. Those had been the days when one knew one's enemy and could fight him face to face, not like nowadays when you didn't know your friend or your foe, like for instance the bureaucrats who had tried to adjust his pension after his wife died. As he stood there in front of the mirror it seemed to him that the helmet made him appear young again, that it gave a sterner cast to his face, till it became like those faces that one saw on coins. As the austere helmeted face gazed back at him from the depths of the glass he thought about those children who ran about outside the house at night and tapped on the windows. It wasn't just mischief, there was evil loose in the world.

The sun was rising and they were all making straight at it. He could hear the big hollow blows of the guns, he could see the earth, continually ploughed beneath him. The sun sparkled from his bayonet and from the bayonets of those to the left and right of him, but he had no time to look who was there, who was still advancing and who was down on the earth. At that very moment his dog would be running across a field, its tongue lolling. On mornings like these he would send him after the sheep, he would be walking about his little empire with his shepherd's crook. But now he was rushing headlong into the blinding sun with a gun and a bayonet in his hand. And they were among the German trenches and there were faces in front of him, some with moustaches, some without. They were all rising like grey rats out of the trenches, the ground was spawning them.

They were . . . He put the helmet back on the sideboard as he heard a knock at the door and there was Elizabeth with his meal. Meals on wheels, they called that. In the old days he wouldn't have accepted charity but now with inflation biting into his pension like a rat there was no reason to be ashamed.

Elizabeth was casting a strange look at the helmet while she poured out some soup for him.

"I've just been feeding Mary Macarthur," she said. "She didn't like the fish. Only Catholics take fish, she told me. You can take your fish away and bring me meat." And she laughed so that her slightly yellow teeth showed.

"Mary Macarthur?" said David as if returning with difficulty to the reality of the village.

"That's right. Up the glen. Of course you know Mary."

"Of course I know Mary Macarthur," said David violently. "Of course I know her. Wasn't I in school with her? She was in the same class as me." He didn't want to tell Elizabeth that his memory sometimes failed him, that often he had to cast about for a name as if he were fishing in a swirling river.

"Of course I know Mary Macarthur. How is she keeping?"

"Oh, she's not too bad. It's mostly arthritis she's got, though she calls it neuritis. I've got the neuritis, she keeps saying."

"Is that right now?" said David complacently, thinking that this young girl did not know about the old. Also she was pale and thin and spectacled and he liked someone with a big hefty body.

"I told her the fish would help her arthritis but she wouldn't take it. It's for the Catholics, my dear, she kept saying. But she gets up and looks after the house. She has a lot of hens, too."

Mary Macarthur: he tried to visualise her. But of course it was Kate's mother, who had been married to Andrew Lang. What was he thinking about? He must have been thinking of the other Macarthur.

Elizabeth was still looking at the helmet and he said, "I took it out to give it an airing."

He finished his soup and began on the fish. How good and rich it was, though his teeth weren't as good as they had once been. He should take a lot of fish to keep him healthy, he would show them yet, he would outlast them all.

"Annie is of course a vegetarian," said Elizabeth. "She won't eat anything but carrots and honey and stuff like that."

How young she was, probably as young as his own grandchild in Australia whom he had never seen, though they were always sending him photographs of her and her parents at Christmas. In his day Christmas Cards were Christmas Cards and had holy verses on them and pictures of angels and fires and coaches and frost, but now people sent you photographs of themselves. Anyway, their Christmas was in midsummer which was ridiculous.

"In the old days," he said, "my wife would take me out my food to the moor."

"Just like Joseph bringing food to the brethren," said Elizabeth brightly. What was she talking about? What had that to do with anything?

"And I would sit and eat it and the sheep would be grazing and my dog would be at my side."

"Is that right?" said Elizabeth. "They don't have many shepherds now."

"No, they don't have much of anything now."

Those sweets that melted like rainbows in one's mouth, they were gone too.

He smacked his lips and said, "That was very good."

Eat, chew, survive, get all the vitamins you can. Outlast them all. Survive, survive. "Did you see the Germans in the Post Office today?" he said.

"No, I wasn't in the Post Office." She gazed at him oddly.

"Well, I can tell you there were Germans there all right. There were two of them and they had cameras."

"Is that right now?" said Elizabeth.

"Yes," he said, "they had fair hair. You can tell them by their fair hair. I'm sure it's that Maisie Campbell that takes them in."

"I never heard," said Elizabeth. "But Greta had Germans for their

Bed and Breakfast last year and do you know what they did? They took all the stuff off the table—the jam, the sugar, everything—and put it all in a bag. Did you hear of anything like that?"

But he was only half listening. They shouldn't be giving rooms to those Germans. Elizabeth was the best of the villagers. Though she was young she was compassionate and they said that she gave most of her wages to Dr Barnardos. She had a good kind heart. In the winter she knitted jerseys for them. What would happen when she got herself a man? And the threat was like a shadow over the room. She and the minister's wife were his best friends in the village, and of course Murdo.

The sun was pouring in through the window and illuminating the bones of the fish left on the plate. But there were no angels to be seen anywhere. Not even Elizabeth was an angel.

She was now tidying everything away. "I'll make you a nice cup of tea," she said, and went into the kitchen. While she ran the water, it was as if for a moment he heard his wife there, the busy ghost that had returned once or twice but only in his mind and in his bed at midnight. Why, in his youth he had beaten her up once or twice and wherever she was she might remember that and not forgive him for it. She had always been asking for jewellery. She could never pass a window without drawing his attention to a ring or bracelet. And yet she had been a good wife too and their last days had been the best and quietest.

"I can't find the sugar," she shouted at him.

He had forgotten to buy any, he really must remember.

"It's all right, I can do without it," he shouted. He was never going to a hospital or home, that was for sure. He had seen the ones who had gone to hospitals, they looked like prisoners of war, and just as helpless.

She came in with the tea and said, "That's the train past. Did you see it?"

"No, I didn't see it."

Maybe she was after his house: maybe that was why she was so kind to him. He could leave her the house if he wanted to. What had his own son and daughter-in-law ever done for him? Except send him photographs of themselves.

No, that couldn't be right, she had a kind heart.

"Do you know what I'm going to do?" she said and before he could stop her she was wearing his helmet. She was parading up and down in front of the mirror trying to make him laugh. His heart almost turned over with the pity of it, the terror of it, her face looked so young and yet so stern with its steel-framed glasses. Her appalling youth frightened him: for a moment there she had looked like an angel, an angel with glasses.

"Do you like me in my helmet with my National Health glasses?" she said laughing.

And he didn't know how to answer her.

Her youth and her clear bones affected him so much that he trembled.

She laid the helmet down on the table and shook her hair out.

"Ah, well, maybe I'll take it up to Mary Macarthur and she can wear it in bed."

She prepared to leave and he said, "I think I'll repair the window today."

"You do that. Keep it up. That's the spirit."

And then she was away again in her small bubbly blue car on an errand of mercy to someone else. She waved to him like an officer from a staff car acknowledging his salute on a morning in France.

The grey cat came and sat on his lap purring contentedly. Its green slanted eyes stared at him unwinkingly while he stroked it. Then he put it down on the floor and said, "Well, cat, I'll have to do something about that window." As he worked he saw Annie heading steadily east on her one mile walk which she took every day except Sunday, her staff in her hand. My God there's a woman for you, he thought, there's a woman for you. As she walked along she beat at the tops of the bushes with her stick and at one point when forced into the ditch by the driver of a racing car turned and waved it furiously and angrily.

8

IN THE MIDDLE of the field little Hugh and Alisdair, guns at their sides, stared at each other. They had worked their way past the Indians and now their wagons were simmering in the sun.

"You go for your gun first," said Hugh.

"No, you go first," said Alisdair. "I'm the sheriff. The sheriff isn't s'posed to go first."

"The sheriff is," said Hugh. There was a wasp humming past his ear and disturbing him. He flicked at it with his hand, keeping his face stern and steady. The wasp zoomed and planed away.

"It's not the sheriff goes first," Alisdair insisted.

"Right," said Hugh. "I'll count up to ten and we both go." And he began to count. "One, two, three," and the wasp returned. Four, five, and he swiped at it again. Bloody wasp, he heard a phantom voice say. Six, seven, and his face tightened. He could feel it tighten. Eight, nine, ten, and he went for his gun, and he saw Alisdair going for his gun and the two of them were staring at each other and Alisdair was shouting, "I beat you, I beat you."

"Bloody wasp," he heard the voice again. No, Alisdair hadn't beaten him. He was stunned by the drench of sun around him, he wanted to run, to dance. "I've got better sandals than you," he shouted. And the larks trilled around him and the bushes flamed with red.

"No, you haven't, you haven't," shouted Alisdair. The wasp had cleared off to wherever wasps went. He should have killed it.

"See," said Hugh and he was bending down and holding a ring in his hand. They stared at it in fascination.

Alisdair tried to take it and Hugh said, "It's mine, it's mine, I found it." He put it in his pocket.

They went and looked at the calf which was feeding in the green, damp grass.

It raised its head and mooed softly.

They saw Mrs Berry coming down with a pail and later the calf burying its hard bony head in the mash. It boxed at the pail, butting at it with its head in its desperate desire to get from it all the sustenance it could. Mrs Berry waved to them as she left the field and closed the gate behind her. She was so very old. The ducks and one drake followed her, tall and disdainful, with their red leathery masks.

Hugh and Alisdair climbed over the fence and descended to the river, which ran green in the half darkness. A rat ran along a bank and they threw stones at it. Then it disappeared through a hole. The day was heavy with scent, their sandals had green blades of grass clinging to them.

They threw stones into the water, creating ring after ring.

9

CHRISTINE MURRAY WAS walking along Byres Road in Glasgow, the message bag in her hand. It was a sunny day sparkling on the glass of windows and cars and she felt around her the perpetual motion of people, as if she were in the centre of a continually flowing stream. Her steps were springier than before, she felt more alive, as if the presence of so many people had animated her and filled her with vigour.

I love him, she thought, he is so unlike John. He lives on the chances of the day. Why, even his betting on horses shows that. Only yesterday he had rushed in and poured money into her lap. You go and buy yourself a coat, he had said, dresses, anything you want. He had looked so confident and young, though he was in fact older than her. She had been out dancing three times and already her village, slow and almost empty, had become only a memory. She had thrown it off with the symbolic casting away of the ring as she had made her way to the railway station in her tall red boots. Nothing would happen to her children, that was certain, John was a good father. Her action had been instinctive, she would never have been able to take it except on impulse, and she was glad that she had done what she did. Now she felt more vigorous, energetic, able to cope with the world around her. They had a flat high above the street and at night she could see the lights from the high rise buildings as if they were becalmed ships in a mysterious sea.

She would get a job in the city soon. When she had settled down, she would perhaps work in an office or a supermarket. She would meet people. Day after day she had lived in the village, waiting for her husband to come home at night, and when he did he had very little to say to her. Terry was different, he was always talking, making plans, it wasn't at all like living in the village, nothing here lasted for too long. In her tall red boots she stopped at a window which showed a silver machine spinning round and round. She went in and found that it was one of those Eastern shops where even the assistants were dressed in foreign clothes. What were they called?

Kaftans? There was a strong smell which was probably incense. There were foods she had never seen before. She felt the centre of attraction. A man in a long coat which trailed behind him glanced at her sideways. There were candles of different colours, a prayer wheel, asses and donkeys in onyx, lighters heavy and solid. The shop was a riot of colours and strange perfumes.

If Terry won more money on the horses she would certainly come in here and buy something. She left the shop and walked up the road, stopping now and then and looking in the windows. It was like Christmas in her mind when she would stay awake all night and finally in the early morning tiptoe in her white cold nightdress across the green linoleum floor, her father and mother still asleep. The city suited her, it was as if she wanted to dance. The light flashing from the windows was like the workings of chance itself. When she stood at corners and gazed at the street it was as if anything could happen to her, as if that boy who had passed in his careless red cape would turn and take her away with him like Batman.

One day she had walked past a cemetery in the city and she had seen people at their midday break sitting among the tombs and eating their sandwiches and playing radios. What an odd experience it had been, and something in her had stirred and been offended by it. There they were lying on the grass or sitting with their backs to the tombstones, some even sitting on the flat ones, drinking their lemonade while their radios played "Sailing". After all it was life and not death that she was interested in.

And now she was going home to the flat high above the street. It was a big spacious flat, not as well furnished as she would have liked, up six flights of stairs past the names of Italians on name-plates outside doors, the circular shaft spinning dizzily below her. If she looked through a window she could see the street with trees growing along it and the cars ranged each behind the other. And at night Terry would come from work in the restaurant where he was a waiter and on Saturday mornings they would roar on his motor bike out of the city. John had met Terry years ago when they had been on a course together in Glasgow where John had been learning about electronics before giving it up and coming back home. Terry had come now and again to see him, having himself abandoned the study of electronics as well.

The three of them used to go out together to the local hotel for drinks and then each time Terry left she had felt an ache in her body that neither John nor the children could assuage. Worst of all she had felt it when she was listening to the radio during the course of the morning and heard the latest songs. It was for instance as if that song "Sailing" had spoken to her, as if it were inviting her to leave her well-ordered life and set off somewhere, anywhere, where there was motion and animation. She had hardly ever been out of the village except when she had been working as a hairdresser in the neighbouring town before she got married. But that hadn't really been like leaving the village. If John had succeeded in electronics they might have moved away but she knew that his heart wasn't really in it and by that time there were the two children and they had been unable to leave. But now she had finally left and she could hear a voice singing, at the back of her mind, "No Regrets", a voice with a French accent and no fear of living.

Even tonight Terry might come home with a few friends and they would put on the radio or some records, and dance. This was what life ought to be like, the unexpected, the random. Or he might take her to the restaurant where he worked and they could have their food there in the half darkness while the juke box played and the wine bottles lay aslant in their baskets and the couples talked gently to each other in the light of candles as if in a TV advertisement. He had told her that it would have taken him too long to make money in the electronics industry. Some day he might become a manager or own a restaurant. After all it was only a question of making contacts, knowing the right people. Before that he had started a sweet-shop which had failed not because of him but because of inflation. Sometimes when he was lying in bed beside her and she watched the lights scissoring the ceiling he would say, "There's so much you can do here. I'd like to have a restaurant which would serve only Scottish food, you know salmon and stuff like that. And I'd have Scottish music and girls in kilts. You could be the manageress." Or he would say, "A bicycle shop might be the best thing to have. Soon there won't be any oil and people will have to ride bikes." Or he would say, "A launderama would be a good bet. Many people don't have washing machines and they can't air their clothes." And she would lie beside him as he talked. The future was a live chancey thing like the smoke that snaked bluely from his cigarette. It was romantic that they should sleep naked in bed. When she had been married to John such a thing had never happened but now it seemed the most natural thing in the world. His mind seethed with ideas like the sun on a loch, he wasn't frightened of the world. However, she had once told him that he smoked too much and he had turned on her. The incident had lasted only a short time, the quick almost insane rage had blown out of the blue and subsided quickly, and then he had been calm again. But that rage had been really vicious, he had been about to strike her. She knew she would have to placate him, there was such a sudden demented strength to his anger.

One day he had shown her the place where he had grown up. It was a slum area which even as she watched was being blown down, men with bluish lights flowering at their gloves, and others high on roofs whistling down at her. In the distance she could see a bridge and then the glitter of the Clyde with the idle cranes dominating the skyline.

She climbed the stairs. Soon she would be in the flat and preparing Terry's food on the gas cooker. She would have much preferred the electric kind to which she was used but it sufficed. And then at night Terry would come home and they would talk and make plans and she herself would decide about a job.

It was an old grey-haired retired schoolmistress who lived opposite them but she herself hadn't spoken to her except that night when she and Terry had asked if they could use her 'phone to call a taxi because the rain was pouring down outside. That was another thing she missed, the 'phone. And the schoolmistress had a chain on her door and then had finally opened it because she recognised Terry and they had paid her the money for the 'phone call. But the schoolmistress had looked at them suspiciously all the time as if she thought they were going to attack her. How lonely she seemed and how lucky she herself was to have Terry! As the taxi made its way among the lights and over the bridge she had clutched Terry's hand while all the time he was saying, "The bugger's taking the long way round, that's for sure." And when he had protested the taxi driver had said, "You can get off here, Jimmy, if you want. It's no skin off my nose, but you pay where you get off," and Terry had snorted angrily but had left it at that. That was the night they had visited his friend Eddie and had stayed there playing records till one o'clock in the morning. Eddie was hunchbacked and collected Space Fiction. "He's a clever lad that," Terry had told her but all she could remember about Eddie was that he smelt, and his rooms were a desolate clutter of books and old boxes as if he were already half packed for somewhere else (perhaps Mars) but couldn't bring himself to go. A budgie jumped restlessly from bar to bar of its cage and preened itself in front of a tiny pink-framed mirror while the hunchbacked Eddie leaned like Humphrey Bogart against a wall.

10

"AND I SAY," said Murdo Macfarlane, "that they shouldn't be given the church hall for their dance."

"And why not?" said the minister patiently.

"Well," said Donald Drummond, pushing back a lock of his silver hair, and not committing himself till he saw what way the minister decided. Murdo's face filled with blood as he tried to put his feelings into words. They were all against him, it was only he that could see the Apocalypse that was coming by giving in to everybody, especially to the younger generation. Drummond always followed the minister, but neither Scott nor Macrae had spoken yet. Scott was the incomer from England who wrote the pantomime every year. As for Macrae he was a slow heavy farmer who had two children of his own.

"It's like this," said Murdo, "the church wasn't meant for dancing in. Where does it say that in the Bible, eh? You tell me that."

The minister stared down at the doodle that he had been pencilling on his note-pad. It seemed to show two angels fighting each other and they had narrow heads like vipers. On the other hand it might just be a pair of birds. The Bible of course could be used to justify anything. In the past he had thought that that was not possible, that he knew the final meaning of all the passages. But what could be made of a saying like, "To them that hath shall be given", or "In my father's house are many mansions"? In what heaven would they sit together round a table such as this holding a committee meeting?

"It certainly doesn't say that in the Bible," said Scott gazing mildly at the minister as if he expected him to make a comment. The minister ignored the look and continued the doodle.

"That's what I am saying," said Murdo triumphantly. "We have to make a stand somewhere."

In the old days if a complaint was made about a postman a form was filled in and if there were no more complaints that year the complaint was scrubbed. But now a postman could put his letters through the wrong letterbox and nothing was done about it. The younger generation didn't care what they did with letters or anything. He for one wasn't giving in to them.

"It doesn't say in the Bible that churches should have church halls," said Macrae slowly. Drummond smiled affably but didn't say anything.

"It's high time we put our foot down," said Murdo angrily. "They think they can get everything they want. Who put them up to this? What did we have when we were growing up? Did we have church halls for dancing? But now they want everything. And who is going to clean it up when they finish, that's another thing I'd like to know."

"I think the janitor might do that," said Scott smoothly. "He's not against it. He's got children of his own."

"And why wouldn't they clean it up themselves?" said Murdo.

"But I thought you were against giving them the hall." Those bloody English, thought Murdo, smooth as oil they are. What's his business here anyway? What right has he to speak?

"The way I see it is like this," said Murdo. "What do they do for the old folk? They're very good at asking but not giving. They expect money just to run a message."

"Oh, I don't think you could say that they don't do anything," said the minister. "The Girl Guides have a party for the Old Age Pensioners. They're not bad children."

"Not bad children? Why are they tapping the windows of the old people's houses at night then? And why are they hanging about the street corners?"

"That's the whole point," said Scott. "It's because they have nowhere to go that they do that."

"It's the devil's work," said Murdo, "that's what I say. They smoke and they drink, some of them. And I'll tell you, I've seen one of them . . ." He stopped suddenly, for the person he was thinking of was Scott's own eldest daughter who had been sent home from a private school because of some scandal.

"What about the school then?" said Macrae slowly. "Why can't we use the school?"

"The school's being used for other things," said Drummond abruptly.

"I can see it all," said Murdo. "You give them this and then they'll ask for something else. They'll want the church itself next. And how many of them go to the Sunday School?"

"I have a class of forty," said the minister without looking up from his note-pad.

"And there's another thing." He stopped. He didn't like putting his wife's proposition next. He felt tired and drained. Well, was it right or wrong to give them the church hall? The fact was that he wasn't sure. Everyone was turning to him for advice as if all the details of dances and church were imprinted in the Bible engraved in letters of stone. The Jews didn't have dances and church halls: that race, at the time the Bible was made, belonged after all to a small section of humanity at a certain stage of development but how could he explain that to the villagers? They would think he was a Communist, all of them except Scott. He was no rabbi equipped with principles from which all deductions easily flowed. For him to speak to them on equal terms they would have to read all the theology that he had himself read, to have suffered what he had suffered.

Of course Murdo was a fundamentalist, as his mother had been. She had even objected when he had given out those little envelopes to put the collection in. They didn't know what demands were made on him all the time from Edinburgh. Did they think about the boat people, the children with large hollow eyes and shrunken bellies in Cambodia, the ships with their cargoes of death? He blinked and his hand trembled. What had this little squabble to do with anything real? He felt himself falling and rising on a nameless grey sea, landing on a strange shore without a name or documents, the brine on his face and body, the yellow-faced guards waiting with their guns poised to blast himself and his companions out to sea again. Anger rose in him like bile. He felt as if he was going to be sick. He steadied himself and took a deep breath and waited it out.

"The thing is," said Scott suavely, "what we have to decide as I see it is, 'was the Sabbath made for man or man for the Sabbath?'" The minister knew what he was getting at but he doubted if the others did.

Poor Murdo was trying to speak again, his face reddening. The minister could understand his point of view: Murdo didn't like the lack of conscientiousness to be found among the young, the fact that they wouldn't take the letters down to the fields rather than hand them over to relatives. But that sort of conscientiousness was surely excessive. He tried to remember what church Murdo's father had gone to but couldn't.

"What we have to decide," said Drummond, "is whether they will look after the hall. That in my opinion is a good part of the question."

Of course that isn't the question, thought the minister, regarding Drummond's burnished face, and silver hair so beautifully waved. That wasn't a theological question, that was only a question of tidiness. The boy and girl who had come to ask him about the hall had been sensible and polite. One in fact was Macrae's daughter and the other Charles Gowan, a widow's son. Their case was quite clear, they felt that they were being deprived of entertainment while the village hall was being repaired.

"I think," he said, putting down his pencil, "that we should put the issue to a vote." The vote was always the easy way out. It only confirmed whether a majority was present for a particular point of view, it didn't guarantee whether that point of view was right.

"Who," he asked, "wants them to have the hall?"

As he expected, both Scott and Macrae put their hands up.

"That leaves it to me," he said. At that moment he thought it might have been much better if he had twenty-four elders as it stated in Revelations, according to Annie. What would she have decided with the wisdom of the East behind her? He smiled wryly and then said, "My casting vote is against giving it to them." Drummond gazed at him with approval while the other two said nothing. It amazed him that he should have done what he had done. When he had said that his was the decisive vote he had no idea what he was going to do. The decision had been made for him at a deeper level than he had himself understood, the Covenanters were still hiding in the brakes of his mind, their voices still spoke through him. It was as if without his knowing it there were voices speaking inside him, voices which without the benefit of a committee had come to a predestined conclusion as if he himself did not exist, as if he were simply a vessel. His face flushed and he would have almost wanted his decision all over again, for like twin railway lines it pointed to a future converging at the horizon in one fixed choice. He looked at the four men, astounded. Had the world begun from tiny drifting molecules so that this committee should be held in this particular room in this particular village? Had Judas been programmed to do as he had done, as Annie had suggested? And why should he, when imminent death should have given him largeness of vision, have denied the hall to the children? But no, in spite of approaching death, there was a heritage to maintain, a gift that flowed through him.

And now it was all over. Scott and Macrae wouldn't hold it against him, he knew that. On the other hand, did he want allies like Drummond and Macfarlane, those echoes of the fundamentalist platitudes?

He knew instinctively that his wife would be against him, for she was on the side of the young. She would have won Murdo and Drummond over to her side: he didn't have the sensitivity or the bonhomie for dealing with people. He rose from the table wishing above all things that he could sit by his fireside and read a book. But, no, he couldn't do that. The real world was always where one was, the kingdom of heaven was at hand. In all decisions great or small the kingdom of heaven was at hand. His stomach felt distended and poisoned. At any moment he was going to be sick.

Murdo waited behind for him as if he wished to be congratulated on the stand he had taken but the minister didn't wish to speak to him. Was Murdo right? Was the Apocalypse near, the wild white horses raging like billows. Were the signs of Sodom and Gomorrah misdirected letters and tappings on windows at night?

"Well, so that's that, Murdo," was all he said as he went out into the sunshine where the gravestones leaned against each other in the slanting light. He saw Mrs Berry bending down, placing a bunch of flowers on her husband's grave. How long since he had died now? Twelve years? Fourteen? And then there was Morag Bheag. He would have to enquire about her son. Mrs Berry straightened and waved to him. Her daughter waited in her yellow car.

The grey gravestones reminded him of the Covenanters, of their determination to worship as they wished. The words stood up in front of his eyes as if engraved on stone:

Blows the wind today and the sun and the rain are flying
blows the wind on the moors today and now

where about the graves of the martyrs the whaups are crying,
my heart remembers how.

Grey recumbent tombs of the dead in desert places,
standing stones on the vacant wine red moor,
hills of sheep and the homes of the silent vanished races,
and winds austere and pure.

He had hardly thought that he knew the words so well. The yellow car, a bright bubble in the day, drew away. The land stretched in front of him, the houses, the gardens, the rivers, the mountain. On such a mountain, but perhaps less green, the tablets had been handed down from a cloud of smoke.

Let me know You again, he prayed, let me hear You speak again. Speak to me out of the fire, the committee meeting, out of the grass at my feet. But, as he looked, the smoke from the different chimneys seemed to twist in different directions like snakes. Where were the martyrs now? In Ireland perhaps where the assassin gunned down the man with the rosary or the fanatic sprayed the policeman with bullets. And in this little place so serene and flowery what could he do? He watched Murdo as he made his way down the brae. He would be happy tonight, the decision would make his day for him. But had he himself made the right decision? He didn't know. Had he really made a decision at all or had he simply responded to the programmed voice of his ancestors, severe and plain, that had spoken through him?

11

"WHAT HAPPENED THEN?" said his wife as the minister came into the manse.

"They're not getting it," he said abruptly.

"Oh? Who decided that?"

"I did."

She was silent for a moment and then said, "Did you mention the picnic, the outing I was suggesting?"

"Not yet."

"I think it would be very nice since the weather is so good," she added enthusiastically. "I see them all in a field as in Biblical times eating their food and drinking their lemonade and the children running their races. The old people must certainly be there. Not just the parents. If necessary we shall provide sandwiches. What do you think?"

"I think it's a good idea."

"Especially," she said, "as the weather is so good and no sign of a break in it. They say that there will be a second crop of fruit. I heard that on the radio. In England, anyway."

"As in 1955," he said.

"1955?"

"It was the same sort of summer. It was the year we came here."

"So it was."

He remembered it very well. It was the year he had left the city and had accepted the charge where he now was. He hadn't believed a place could be so beautiful. He had walked about in a daze of happiness. Why, the very stones seemed to be shining as in a Revelation of their own. One morning he had seen a fawn feeding at the side of the manse, its delicate face twitching. The two of them had gazed at each other as if across an earth that was touched with annunciation. Even the stained glass windows had sparkled with their pictures of shepherds with staffs, the Christ figure holding out its empty hands, pale and bearded.

"Don't you remember?" he said.

"Yes, I remember."

In those days he had lived as in Nazareth or in Bethlehem. On Easter Sunday when he saw all the women in church with their new hats it was as if his heart turned over with pain and pleasure. Mrs Cameron, the organist, filled the stone building with music and it was only afterwards that he had been disturbed by the small mirror which she had in front of her. She tidied her hair at it before beginning to play.

"I wonder if Bach did that," he had thought rapturously.

His two boys would come home in the evening in their football boots and muddy jerseys and he himself as if enchanted would read his commentaries and prepare his sermons in a continual trilling of birds.

He suddenly grasped his wife's hand and they stood there in the living room in the autumn twilight. Soon the moon would rise, startlingly brilliant, and the millions of stars would come out as if engraved on the sky.

His wife said, "I don't like Morag Bheag's son being in Ireland."

"Have you seen Annie? She'll have something to say about it."

"No, I haven't seen her."

"She's interested in the East now," he said. "She'll end up as a Hindu or a Mohammedan. She believes that all the wisdom of the world came from there."

"Is that right? Of course she's a funny woman. But strong."

"She's strong certainly. One of these days she'll go about in a veil. I believe she has dismissed her Jehovah's Witness."

"I would imagine that. Are you feeling all right? You look pale."

"I'm fine. It's just those silly committee meetings."

They sat there companionably while the moon rose ahead of them, shedding its uniform predestined light.

"Do you believe," he said, "that everything is predestined?"

"I thought we had gone through all that already. I don't and neither do you."

"Sometimes I wonder about it," he sighed. "I feel as if I have been here before, as if my whole life is a replay of an earlier recording."

"Even your committee meetings?"

"Especially these," he answered, smiling.

"I feel as if I'm catching up on what has already happened. And yet I shouldn't feel like that. The truth about Christ was that He was new, that He gave the world a fresh start. The rest of us pass on our weaknesses and our sins, only He was pure." He was silent for a moment and his wife said, "I don't believe the gift shop will sell very much. I was in again today and there were only two people there. Why they should have opened a gift shop I don't understand."

"Are there many tourists?"

"Oh, plenty. Germans, Dutch, and even two Japanese."

"Japanese?"

"I believe he's an engineer. He's got a tiny wife and a tiny child, and he stays with Calum the butcher. You know that his wife does bed and breakfast."

"I know.

"Sometimes," he said, "I wonder what my contribution to this place has been. What should the job of a minister be? Maybe it should be to disguise death from them? Or go about in a hairshirt. At least the people who provide tourists with bed and breakfast know what they are doing."

"You look thin enough for a saint," his wife said affectionately.

He heard the train's whistle and was again reminded of predestination. Maybe they should go and visit one of their sons. In fact he ought to visit both of them before anything serious happened to him. Immensely pure, the moonlight swam about them. Endure, endure, as the Anglo Saxons had done among the storms and the blizzards when their castles where they had been happy had been taken away from them. What was that poem again about Maldon? 'While the spirit endures.'

"The cat caught a vole today," said his wife dreamily. "I found it in the garden with it. I took it out of its mouth and released it. It was playing with it on the lawn."

"Good," he said absently. He wondered where the cat went during the day. It left the house every morning and padded into the bushes with a sense of purpose and then in the evening it sat by the fire humming to itself like a hoover.

Even the cats had purpose.

"Young Hugh and young Alisdair found a ring," said his wife, "near the railway station. They brought it home to Calum. His wife thinks it belonged to Chrissie Murray."

"Oh? Did she lose it?"

"They think she might have thrown it away when she was going to catch the train. It's the sort of thing she might do. She wanted to be finished with it all perhaps."

"And so she threw the ring away?"

"That's the theory anyway. A ring wouldn't normally fall from one's finger."

"I hope John doesn't find out."

"They're not going to give it to him. I think they might give it to you so that you can keep it. They think you are wise and will know what to do."

There it was again, the childish trust that the Bible had something to say about women who left their husbands, taking transistor radios with them, and throwing rings into bushes. He, their minister, wasn't any wiser than they were. Sometimes he thought that Kenny Foolish who wandered about the village with his big blank clock-face was just as wise as he was himself, and with whom little children played contentedly for he was a child himself and as much as them would play games for hours together.

"I don't mind keeping it," he said. "I don't think John should see it. He's got enough on his plate. And in any case we don't know definitely that it was Chrissie's."

"It is more difficult for a man to be left alone to cope," said his wife mildly.

It came into his mind how a minister from a town he knew had taken a little Vietnamese child into his house. There she sat, gentle and smiling, after the helicopters had burned her village with waves of flame. O world, what is happening to you? Is there no one listening while the Irish gun each other down from speeding cars, while the boat people rise and fall on blank nameless seas, while millions of children hold out shrunken arms in Cambodia? Sorrow and grief without end, and how little he knew of it. He had never been starved, he had never been nearly drowned, he had never been burned with napalm. What then had he to say?

"I think I'll go to bed," he said. "I feel tired." Her sharp eyes clouded for a moment and he could have sworn that she knew what was wrong with him, but she didn't say anything. My bonny little fighter, he thought, you stood out for me even when I tried to shift the blame, you've been as straight as a die. And yet you are infinitely mysterious to me, your womanly ways are strange and odd like a river that sings in the night. I don't understand you, your concern for cups and plates and chairs. Do not think of the morrow, do not lay up treasure on earth, for the moth will corrupt it.

He saw the lights go out in Calum's house and then in Collins' house and then in Mrs Berry's house.

"I'll come to bed as well," said his wife, "after I've locked up."

He was suddenly almost consumed with rage. I'm the fig tree without fruit, so much to do and so little time or inclination to do it. Give me a sign, he murmured inwardly, give me a sign, O Lord. But the moon shone, bright and distant, and he thought with astonishment, men walked on that brilliant barren globe. The Universe swarmed with people. If he himself had been born in Cambodia what would he have been? Would he have confronted the teeming jungle with his starched collar?

His wife came in and they entered the bedroom together. She sat in front of the mirror for a moment loosening her hair. Dear girl, he thought, I love you. I shall love you forever even in death. And he shivered. He heard the throaty cry of an owl as it quartered the woods searching for a mouse, a vole, anything that moved. The berries had lost their redness in the dark. A dog howled and then a cat as if caught in barbed wire suddenly screamed. The sky was a sieve of a million lights, space was endless. He felt suddenly dizzy and sat down on the bed. We twa hae paiddlt in the burn. The words came into his mind and were infinitely sad and regretful. His wife turned to him in her white nightgown and they clutched each other in the darkness. "I'll turn over now," she said and kissed him. Her kiss was fragrance on his lips. He imagined Judas bending down and lightly touching with his lips the divine face in the shroud. The pulpit was a forest full of complications. How had he ever thought that he had understood what he had been doing?

12

MARY MACARTHUR LISTENED to John Murray working on the roof
which was being repaired because it let the rain in during the winter.
She hoped that he wasn't a Catholic. Ever since her daughter Kate
had married that fellow Danny Young she hadn't liked Catholics.
Her grandchildren were going to be brought up in the Catholic
Church even though she had raised Kate up to be a faithful Protestant, sending her to Sunday School in her twin ribbons of red,
teaching her to recite passages of the Bible such as that section about
Charity from Corinthians which her father had taught her himself
when she was a child. But there had been no way of stopping Kate
from marrying, she had been set on it, and now she would pay for it
with holy water and candles and vulgar incense.

Actually it was possible that the whole village was seething with
secret Catholics pretending to be Protestants when they were not.
One couldn't put anything past them. She wasn't sorry when she
heard that the chapel had been broken into, that would teach them.
And look at all the trouble they were causing in Ireland with their
masks and their guns. My poor Kate, she thought, when I hoped you
were going to be a comfort to me in my old age, look what
happened, you were taken in and deceived by smooth words. And
anyway Danny Young's mother was a dirty woman incapable of
keeping her house spick and span. And on top of that she smoked, at
her age. What could you expect of people like that?

When her daughter came to visit her it was as if she had been let out
on parole. Of course she now knew that she had made a mistake but
she wouldn't admit it. She was too proud to tell her own mother that
she was like a prisoner of war. Look at what they did to their
womenfolk in Belfast, they tarred and feathered them and shaved
their hair.

She put the kettle on and went outside and shouted to the joiner to
come down. He was a nice fellow, name of Murray, and his wife had
run away with another fellow. A Catholic, she shouldn't wonder.

They were everywhere in Glasgow, the city was hoaching with them. Leaving him with those two little girls, it wasn't right, nothing good would come of it. Murray was very quiet these days. In the early days you would hear his whistling as he worked but he didn't whistle now. He came inside, his ruler in the top pocket of his dungarees and sat down in the chair that she had placed at the table for him. She had laid out a roll and tea for him. He said, "It's just as well that you did the roof just now. The rain would be in in the winter."

She felt even as he spoke the stabbing pain in her hip. Actually she wouldn't put it past that doctor to be a Catholic as well. Sometimes she wondered whether she shouldn't throw away the pills he gave her though the pain was great. He didn't belong locally, that was sure, and Stewart was a Catholic name. A lot of tinkers were called Stewart as well. Murray ate his roll quietly and drank his tea, as if he didn't wish to speak, or as if he had nothing to speak about. He looked drained and blank. Why, she could remember when his children had been baptised in those days when she could go to church and didn't have to stay in the house all the time.

She didn't know whether she ought to mention his wife. Sympathy was good for a man, but on the other hand he might not wish to talk about it.

"I'll tell you," she said abruptly, "my own son-in-law should have done that roof for me, but these Catholics can't do anything. He didn't need to have been told about it. He could have climbed that roof with a ladder. Why couldn't he do that? The priest maybe told him not to, because I'm a Protestant. He doesn't care whether I have water coming in and ruining my good wallpaper."

Murray had become morose right enough. He had finished his roll and was making himself a cigarette. She had heard that if you gave workers tea they would add it to the time that they had been on the job, but she didn't think that Murray was like that. She chattered on while he smoked.

"Of course," she said, "they usually have big families and that's why they are poor. The Pope makes them have a good family and yet he's not married himself. That's to make sure that there are more of them than of us. He came to Ireland and told them all to have big families. He landed there in a 'plane. I'll tell you another thing, he's a

Communist. They think he's descended from St Peter, but Peter was a true Protestant and anyway you never found any of the disciples travelling about in 'planes. They were given a little food and they were told to go about the world preaching. That's what Christ said to them. Now they have council houses."

As he sat at the table silently she thought that perhaps he ought to have married Kate. He had always been a good clean worker and look what happened to him: there was no justice in the world. If there was, how should a good workman who had harmed no one be shamed like that, in front of his own people. He should have taken a whip to that wife of his with her bare knees and her red boots. In fact she thought that she remembered him having been out once with Kate but she wasn't sure about that. Kate had been out with so many boys before she got married. One of them had given her a beautiful ring and hadn't even asked for it back when she got married to someone else.

"Thanks for the tea," he said, looking for an ashtray in which to stub his cigarette. She laid a blue one on the table and said, "You're welcome." He was looking very thin as if he didn't eat much. It was different for a man, men couldn't look after themselves in the same way as women could. She wondered if anyone washed his dungarees for him.

"I'll tell you," she said, "that man from Glasgow is a Catholic, you mark my words." He winced and half smiled. "Don't you believe that he isn't. Look at Danny Young. He's married to my own daughter and he works in a garage. What does he know about repairing cars? He never had any training in his life. When was he ever a mechanic? Where are his certificates?" He stared at her as if he was going to cry, his face so pale. It wasn't right, no it wasn't right, and she didn't care who heard her. One flesh the Bible said, one flesh and everything held in common.

He stood up and said, "Well, I'd better be getting back to my work."

Day followed day and it was difficult to get up in the morning, especially if one had no one but oneself. She put her hand on his shoulder as if he were a small boy and said, "Never mind, I'm an old woman and nothing good will come of it." He turned away and later she heard him hammering on the roof. She put out some bread for the little birds that came to the bird box that her husband had made. She sniffed the wide morning air: every day was blue and began with mist which later cleared away. God looked after even his own sparrows but you found it was the buzzards that had the best of it.

The air was very still, apart from the hammering, and she could see the smoke rising from the houses, drifting away in the direction of the railway line. She should have asked someone to paint her door which was a dull green. She looked up as the hammering continued and saw him sitting astride the roof, a clutch of nails in his mouth.

13

"Look," said Alisdair to Hugh and he pointed to the grey cat—it belonged to David Collins—which was carrying a baby rabbit in its mouth across the railway line. It padded along, looking neither to right nor to left, its fat body heavy and smoky, as if it was filled with grey water.

They followed it across the rusty rails, among the wet grass which left green threads on their sandals. It stopped and looked when it heard them approaching. They stared into its fathomless eyes which seemed so calm and deep and mysterious, like emeralds. The sun sparkled on the stones, there were berries on the trees. It was a morning of intent serenity, and through it as if through a picture the cat padded.

Suddenly Alisdair began to run and Hugh ran after him. The cat scampered up the brae but the boys were close behind it. Alisdair began to pick up stones and throw them. The cat looked behind it again and sped onward. A stone hit it in the back and it winced. Alisdair ran ahead to cut off its progress, before it could reach David Collins' house. It dodged hither and thither but, caught between the two boys, it didn't know what to do. Its eyes flashed but it still clamped the rabbit in its jaws. On such a fine morning it seemed to be wondering about the injustice of the world, when all it was doing was hunting for its daily food. Alisdair had got hold of a branch and was pushing the cat back, thwacking the ground with it. As if defeated the cat laid the rabbit down, then sped between the boy's legs and ran away.

"Is is okay?" said Alisdair breathlessly. They picked the rabbit up. And stroked it. Its little body heaved.

"We'll let it go," said Alisdair.

"Don't be stupid," said Hugh, "it wouldn't live."

He had once seen his mother stopping the car and picking up a wounded bird and placing it in cotton wool which she had taken from an aspirin bottle. Its beak had pecked at her feebly.

"That's right," said Alisdair, "it wouldn't. I'll take it home."

"No, I'll take it home," said Hugh. "My father knows about rabbits. He's a butcher."

Alisdair whose father was dead didn't say anything, but he too felt injustice. After all it was he who had saved the rabbit. But they didn't have a hutch at home and probably Hugh had. They had everything because they were well off.

The tiny rabbit panted in Hugh's hand.

"If you like," said Alisdair carelessly as if he didn't wish Hugh to know that he too had been wounded and hurt.

Hugh went on ahead with the rabbit in his hands, a hero coming home from the wars. Alisdair knew that Hugh would gain the credit for saving the rabbit and the tears pricked his eyes. In his mind's eye he saw the calm fathomless eyes of the cat. When Miss Lamond had strapped Hugh, his father had been at the school the following day but when he himself had been strapped his mother refused to go. "You probably deserved it," she had said. And later, "You have to learn to take your punishment." David Collins shouted "Hello" to them as they passed. He was an old man and he had a big red nose, with hair in his nostrils and his ears.

14

WHILE HALF LISTENING to his wife the Reverend Peter Murchison was thinking of a time when he had been travelling on the train home from Glasgow. It had been a winter's night and he had been reading in his compartment when he suddenly looked up from his book and there, across the water, across the Clyde, he had seen the lights of the houses and the shops and the cinemas and the restaurants. Immediately there they were, columns of green and red and white towering almost solidly upside down into the water, so that the town, composed of tenements, suddenly became opulent and colourful, almost Eastern in its dazzle of pillars. Then as he still stared in astonishment he saw a curving snakelike yellow apparition of lights and then—darkness.

"And Mrs Scott objected," said his wife, "on the grounds that it might be a wet day. I told her that if it was we could always make use of the sandwiches and lemonade. In any case we always used to have a Sunday School picnic every year, I said, and we had to take that risk. But I don't think it's much of a risk this year."

"Of course not, dear," said the minister.

"She then asked who was going to pay for it and I said that some of the women had agreed to make the sandwiches and as for the lemonade we could maybe hold a small Sale of Work to raise the money. It wouldn't need much organising."

"I see," said the minister.

"Of course if she had thought of the idea herself . . . I mean having the old people as well," said his wife, "she would have been all for it. But she's a good worker and I'll have to convince her that she did think of it herself."

"That's a good idea."

Opposite him on top of the bookcase he saw the Spanish doll which his wife had bought some months before. It stood on thin legs, dressed in a pink frock and flaring pink skirt with a pink flower in its long dark hair which streamed over the shoulders. He imagined it on top of a grave in a cemetery.

There had been Mrs Sinclair the old widow who had lived by herself and refused to let anyone into her house. Eventually she had no lighting and no heating, her corridor was full of empty bottles, the ceiling had collapsed and fallen on the bed and Mrs Sinclair had lived in that squalor for day after day till she had died. The beached detritus of bottles and dirt and papers had taken four days to shift. He imagined the doll standing on her grave and crowing like a cockerel.

"That's right, dear," he told his wife, "you handle that. You're more diplomatic than me." And indeed she was. He himself couldn't come to terms with the ordinary contradictions of life, and life, he was beginning to believe, was all contradictions, immune to reason.

"When were you thinking of holding the Sale of Work?" he said, taking out his diary.

"I think perhaps in a fortnight's time," she said, "say August the ninth and then have the picnic the following Saturday."

His wife of course could see the contradictions better than he could but she could live among them without being greatly affected. On the other hand if there was no predestination why should he object to the contradictions? How could he object to both? How could he object to rails and the absence of rails at the same time? But then religion was not a reasonable thing and neither was life. He felt the pain stab at him again and winced.

"Is there anything wrong, dear?" said his wife.

"A touch of indigestion." Bearing this pain was like feeling a child growing within one. It was an obscure pregnancy unlooked for, evil, irreversible, a punishment perhaps for an unwillingness to accept the contradictions. She was looking at him with concern.

"Would you like a cup of coffee or anything?"

"No, dear, I'll be all right. So it's August the ninth then," and he put his diary away.

"The thing about Mrs Scott," said his wife, "is that being an outsider no one has accepted her. She has lots of ability but her accent puts people off. And then Mrs Campbell is rather busy now with her Bed and Breakfast."

"Yes, of course."

And then he added, "You can take the paperbacks to the Sale of Work."

"All of them?"

"Yes you can take all of them. We need the space anyway."

"If you're really sure . . ."

His wife of course didn't read as much as he did. He had always been a reader. In that ideal kingdom he had spent most of his days. It came to him with a pang that few people read books at all, that he was an exception, that most people's lives were circumscribed by their daily work. The love of beauty and reading came from that excess energy that was left over from existing.

One of the terrible revelations that had come to him as a minister was hearing a woman—who had it been? Mrs Scott herself perhaps or Mrs Campbell?—saying to Kate in a shop,

"Of course, dear, she wore the same hat as she wore last week. Has she nothing else to wear?"

At that moment he had a comic yet tragic vision of God as a dress designer staring down from heaven with a considering eye on the blouses, hats and coats of the congregation, assigning them to heaven or hell according to the quality and newness and brilliance of their clothes. How far one could go from the centre of the truth to trivial trumpery mirrors!

"I think," said his wife, "that I'll talk to Mrs Berry's daughter, Patricia. She can help me with the cakes and things."

"I'm sure she will," said the minister.

He watched her affectionately as she got up from the chair, kissed him lightly on the cheek, waved to him and then busily entered her car and sped cheerily down the drive. What would happen to her when he died? It was better, he supposed selfishly, for her to survive than for him to do so. How dependent he had been on her all his life! It was as if without her he didn't exist at all. Perhaps that was what love was, the dread of the other's absence, the dread of her extinction, a match being put out in the dark.

Through the window in front of him he could see old Smelly who lived in a cave by himself (he was at that very moment bending over to peer into a big yellow bin) and who came out of it each morning in his long unutterably dirty coat that trailed the ground, to poke among the scraps of food that others had thrown out. On an impulse he walked down to where Smelly was and as he did so he imagined with loathing the rats simmering in the bin among the damp biscuits, fragments of bread, empty milk cartons, shoes with no laces, mounds of tins.

Smelly raised his gaunt unshaven face towards him when he saw him coming.

"How are you, sir?" he said through his black broken teeth.

"Fine, fine, Mr Morrison," said the minister. "And how are you yourself?"

"No complaints," said Smelly who was holding a big canvas bag in his hands and putting bits of bread and biscuit into it as he spoke. His unwashed coat trailed the ground. The hem of my garment has been touched, some virtue has gone out of me, thought the minister. Not far from them a buzzard waited, and a small group of seagulls. The long thin veined hand stretched into the bin. The horror, the horror, thought the minister, what if a rat should suddenly clamp it fast. His eyes closed at the thought of it and he swayed momentarily, feeling dizzy. How is it you live and what is it you do? The old leech gatherer on the moor, the wanderer, half stone, half man, the murmur of the Presbyterian voice.

"Fine weather," said Smelly, briskly filling his bag as calmly as if he were out shopping.

"It is that, Mr Morrison," said the minister, "no sign of rain at all."

Smelly, strangely enough, had a beautiful voice and when he was drunk on VP as he so often was, when he could get it, he would sing opera and sentimental Scottish songs, marching up and down like a retired soldier, his mouth frothing. Once the minister had seen him following David Collins like an obscene shadow from the First World War marching behind him, imitating him. It was fatal to give him money for then he would follow one, thanking one, especially if he was drunk. He probably slept in a cave, or a barn for sometimes his clothes were prickled and veined with straw: his boots of course were windowed with holes. Today however he was sober, un-ashamed, at ease. No one knew where he had originally come from. It was said that he had trained as a musician and then a love affair had left him stranded on the shore from which he could see the ships of other more successful crews.

He packed his bag with what he could find in the bin. In one of the open tins the minister could see a few clotted beans. Once he had passed the bin in his car and had seen a goose—a white angel—stretching its long pure neck into it.

On an impulse and well aware of the danger he took a fifty pence piece from his pocket and gave it to Smelly.

"And don't spend it on drink," he said.

"On drink," said Smelly, his face breaking into a smile as if an old rock with its green wet moss had suddenly shone wetly. "Me, sir, spend it on drink? I wouldn't spend it on drink, sir." Was there a hint of an Irish accent there?

"It's for food," said the minister, "remember that." Perhaps he ought to have someone like Smelly in the church, to let him walk the aisle among the women in their green and red and blue hats, interwoven with flowers. And what if Smelly did come in, smelling of drink, singing his drunken operatic arias, his mouth dripping with foam, and they all would walk out? Did they have the right to?

He stood there feeling ashamed of himself. Oh, God, he prayed silently, who gave us Your beautiful day with the larks trilling in the heavens, the buzzard sitting on his fence post, the seagull alert and ravenous, the trees with their blood-red berries, how can I not feel Your grace?

Sometimes he and his wife would go and collect bramble berries, stretching their hands out among the thorns. Why was it that the best berries were always protected by thorns? The two of them wore wellingtons and gloves and placed their plunder in bags, just as Smelly was doing now.

He saw a soggy slice of bread disappearing down the open tunnel of Smelly's sack and almost vomited on the spot but Smelly was by then seriously examining an old boot.

"Too small," he muttered to himself as the minister had seen his own wife doing at a bargain sale. What is it that you do and how is it you live?

Some people claimed that Smelly stole eggs from the barns, but Smelly maintained that it was the foxes who did that, the cunning-faced innocent thieves. Was it Smelly who had killed Mrs Robertson's hens whose heads and necks had been found one morning, white with frost, outside the henhouse, though there was nothing left of the bodies but a few brown feathers?

Smelly was finished. His bag over his shoulder he was beginning to move off, a hobo into the blue.

"Thank you for the money, sir," he said, tipping his rancid cap.

"God bless you," said the minister. For a moment he had an overwhelming desire to speak to Smelly and they stared at each other quivering with the warm dialogue that could have gone on between them, that would leave them naked to the day, but the instant passed and Smelly moved on towards his cave and his breakfast.

Once he turned and waved, and the minister was still standing by the bin. Maybe he could get a sermon out of this, how we put our sins in hiding for the rats to gnaw at, how we are a chest of orts and fragments, a treasury of scurrying guilts and shames, how the bitten apple cores of our lives lie in the darkness, how the seagulls feed on them, the seagulls with their wide white wings and blood-flecked beaks. The angels who refuse nothing, whose gaze is intent and voracious.

He turned home towards his study.

15

As DAVID COLLINS was standing at the gate he saw the German coming towards him. Spectacled and wearing shorts, the visitor had a fishing rod in his hand; his hair was closely cropped.

"I am not moving from here," thought David. "Why should I? This is my country. This is my village. What is he doing fishing in our rivers anyway? Who does he think he is? I shall speak to him."

The German was wearing boots and his legs looked thin and meagre. He also wore a peaked green cap which was probably to keep the sun out of his eyes.

"They come here and they think they own the place. Where is he staying anyway? It's probably with Maisie Campbell."

He trembled with excitement and fever. His heart beat fast and his hand was hot and sweaty on the gate, but like a sentry who refuses to give up his post even in the middle of danger he waited stubbornly. The sun above him was golden and round in a perfectly blue sky. Out of the morning sunlight the German came and it was as if his green cap became a grey helmet, thorny and vicious, and the rod in his hand was like a rifle pointing at David's heart.

To be old was shameful, to feel the heart hammering in one's breast as if it were trying to break free of the cage of flesh and bone: to feel oneself so often wishing to urinate, unable to contain one's water. All that was humiliating. The German was very close to him now. He would stare at him and then go back into the house. He owed himself at least that, he owed it to all the others who were dead in those fields so far away, he owed it to Iain, to William, and all the rest whose names were engraved on the village memorial. The German stopped in the pouring innocent sunlight and faced him. "Good morning, sir," he said and for a moment David was confused. It wasn't so much that the German had spoken to him, it was rather that he had called him "sir" as if he were an officer, for the officers were those who strolled, sticks in hand, about parade grounds or were seen waving elegantly from staff cars, distant, clean, smiling, and falsely encouraging. The German looked quite young, not more than forty, and his glasses flashed in the sun. His expression was polite and enquiring and he stood there in front of David like an overgrown schoolboy slightly ridiculous in his shorts, his knees so plainly white. "He doesn't have the legs for the kilt," thought David. "He looks like a scholar. The rod seems new. He wouldn't have been much use in the trenches." The German was standing awkwardly in front of him and saying, "I am going to fish." He spoke very distinctly and looked anxious as if afraid that he would not be understood. Without his knowing exactly that he was doing it David pointed towards the river and said, "Over there. The river's there." He spoke to the German as if he were addressing a child. The German's eye obediently followed where he pointed. Many a time he himself had fished in that river bringing home trout in the evening, dipping his rod in the shadows, watching the circles widening as the midges bit at the backs of his hands.

"Thank you," said the German standing there awkwardly. What did he want to know now? When it came to the point he couldn't not speak to him. His loneliness and good manners had betrayed him, he could not after all stand there and outstare the German and he was angry with himself. What did good manners have to do with war? Had the Germans been good-mannered on mornings such as these, the glaring sun rising ahead of them as they charged.

"Good fish there?" said the German on a rising note, fitting the words together carefully as if each were a stone to be selected with the greatest care.

"Yes," said David, "the fishing is good," though he hadn't been to that river now for many years. His rod was in the shed at the bottom of the field and he never touched it now. So also was his gun.

"Thank you," said the German again tipping his green cap, and then he was on his way while David gazed after him. From the back the German looked even more ridiculous than he had from the front, meagre and thin, a plucked chicken.

"I shouldn't have spoken to him," thought David. "I should have ignored him. I should have stared at him and let him know that he is my enemy, that he was my enemy. But I was too weak and lonely." He had an impulse to go and shout names after him as children sometimes did with Kenny Foolish if they were feeling in a cruel mood. He would say, "Why did you kill William and Alisdair then? Why did you try and kill me? I was a shepherd and suddenly I found myself in the filthy trenches. There was one time I pulled a pair of boots off a German whose body was hanging on the wire. His face was green but his boots were serviceable. One thing you could say for them, they produced good stuff." And now that German was going down to the river, to fish in his water, to sit there quietly in the water, and cast his rod for his trout. Was there no end to their impudence?

But, then, thank God there was nothing wrong with his eyesight. He could still recognise a German when he saw one.

And at that moment a pure intense feeling pierced him as if it were the taste of the strawberries that he had once stolen from the schoolmaster's garden on a day perhaps exactly like this many years ago. It was as if his shoes were peeled from him and he was running on his bare feet towards that same river to which the German had gone, and he and William were dipping their hands into the water in search of the small fish that glanced about it. The shadows from the trees that lined the bank overhung them and he could see quite clearly the network that they cast on William's face. He could see the pair of white legs trembling, askew in the water, and he could hear a lark singing in the sky, and his own heart ran over with happiness. He heard himself shouting and though he couldn't make out the words he knew he was speaking and then the two of them were out of the water and dashing along the bank avoiding any sharp stones that they saw, and in search of the nest from which the lark had sprung so suddenly and so piercingly. The two of them were now staring down at the speckled eggs, touching them lightly with their fingers, feeling them warm and inexpressibly delicate, William's head beside his own, fragile and tousled, his eyes open with wonder: they were on their knees and their feet wet and the parts between their toes muddy. It was the greatest, most radiant, morning of the world and it was as if his heart had stopped for he felt it and not only saw it, and the gush of its advent was heartbreakingly pure. The eggs were so small, so vulnerable, it was as if the two of them were gods with the power of life and death, the world was so open and so fragile, so full of marvels, the sun so hot on their speckled wrists which seemed to echo the freckles on the eggs. It was a treasury to which there was no end, it would always be like this, compact of mornings such as these, which one opened like a box, so strongly scented with the most airy perfumes. The small heart beat in his aged breast, like the lark that had now fallen silent. They had turned away from the nest, and now they were running past the tree with the trembling quick green leaves, dancing in light and in shade, and the sun, a golden eye in its socket, and then it all suddenly changed and it was his wife who was saying, "That box with the powder puff now." Her eyes were turned on him, faithfully demanding, she had had so little in her whole life: her poverty, echoing his own, made him angry because he couldn't relieve it. A cloud passed over the day, the pools darkened, her eyes dulled, the fish slid under the bank, and the sockets became gaunt and old. They stared at him out of the box, the matron was putting her hands in his, and his whole body was shaking with a ruined emptiness.

He shook his head like a dog emerging from water with a stone in its mouth and the world steadied again to the habitual landscape which confronted him.

16

"OF COURSE," SAID Mrs Scott to her husband, "They've never really accepted us. That's just an example, the refusal to lease the church hall."

"I wouldn't exactly say that," said her husband, "not exactly." He was of course Capricorn and she Taurus and the Capricorns were the quietly persistent ones, ambitious, determined, hard-working, as Gerald had been all his days as bank manager in Surrey and now retired to this village. Taurus people on the other hand were flesh-centred, faithful and constant, and liable to butt their heads at gates.

"The fact is," he said calmly, "they think differently from us. Their priorities aren't ours."

"What priorities?" she asked, placing in the sink the coffee cups from which they had just drunk.

"Well, they preserve their links with the past in a way that we don't. We have to remember that. And in any case I don't think Mr Murchison is well."

"What's wrong with him?"

"I don't know. I just have that feeling. I've been noticing him recently in the pulpit. He's a good man, you know."

"Of course. I'm not saying that he isn't. But this idea of having a sort of outdoor feast is ridiculous. It's like the loaves and the fishes. And then holding a Sale of Work to pay for it."

"At least they're trying, you must admit that they try, that they're go-ahead."

"If you say so. Sometimes I wish we had never come here in the first place."

"I think you're in a mood, that's all. It will pass."

"You admit yourself that they're different from us. One of them hinted to me the other day, it was that woman Campbell, would you believe what she said to me? She asked me if my father and mother were buried in England and when I said yes she more or less implied that she couldn't understand that sort of barbarism. That I could leave them there. Imagine that."

"I can imagine that," said her husband quietly. "Strangely enough, I can understand it. You see, they are used to deriving their strength from the dead. I saw the minister doing that. I think he himself was surprised that he made the decision that he in fact made. For a moment I thought that he would go the other way but his psychology prevented him from doing so. It was very interesting. It was as if another voice spoke through him and he was in the power of a ventriloquist."

"What voice?"

"I think the voice of his ancestors. That's the only way I can explain it. But he did look ill. He was sweating a lot. There's something wrong with him."

"Why isn't he in his bed then?"

"I don't know. I'm not sure that it's wholly physical. You see, there are strains on a minister that we don't understand."

"Fiddlesticks. It's a job like any other job."

"No, it's not, Martha. It's not a job like any other job. In England one might think the clergy had forgotten their roots, the holiness of their calling. But there's something thistly here, and something you can get a grip of though it pricks you."

"How holy for instance is Annie then?" said his wife plumping herself down on the sofa beside him.

"Oh, that's different. She doesn't fit and she's looking for a cage."

She stared at him blankly.

"A cage?" she echoed.

"Yes. We all need a cage. We can't be allowed to be free. It's not good for us."

Certainly after leaving the bank himself he had felt the terrors of freedom for a long time though he was reconciled to them now. They didn't peer out at him from unexpected corners as they had done in the past with their hollow haunting eyes. Which was why he couldn't understand someone like that Murray girl for instance making such a daring leap into the void. She interested him. His own life had been one of routine all his days, clocking in at nine in the morning, leaving at five in the evening, staring through the grille at faces at times delirious with guilt and despair. No, he couldn't understand that girl and yet when he thought of her some deep sorrow moved in him, as if he had missed in that clean office the fertile bacteria of existence. He imagined her as young and hopeful, casting her rope off, setting off into the blue, a sex-stricken and trampish waif. What had been her thoughts as she had left, that day, as she had made her way through the fields to the train, as she had boarded it, radio in hand? Often he himself had felt like taking the startling leap but he had never had the courage to do it. He had remained in the net, however much his wings had quivered for elsewhere.

"I don't understand what you're talking about," said his wife briskly. "Sometimes I think you are becoming as demented as the rest of them."

He smiled carefully as if he were putting on a face to a customer, drawing him politely into his little office, sitting opposite him, alert and helpful on his swivelling chair.

He felt sorry for his wife that she was not accepted truly into the community, that she was like a newcomer to an old school, always on the edge of things, and because she was being too brash, too opinionated. Would she never learn that this was the home of the villagers, that they were what they were, and that it was she who must change? Why had she objected to Mrs Murchison's gathering in the open air? There was something imaginative and Biblical about it. She had only objected to it because she felt she ought to, not because there was anything wrong with the idea itself. He felt protective towards her but at the same time baffled by her almost invincible stupidity.

"I think," he said in the same calm voice, "that we could find stuff for the sale if we looked carefully enough, and that we should try to adapt more. We should listen more and talk less."

"Why should I?" said his wife aggressively. "After all if we were living in Surrey people would pay attention to me. Why should it be any different here? The points I made were fair. I only said that it might rain on the day and that the project would be expensive, providing lemonade not only for the Sunday School children but for adults as well. Quite apart from the food."

It was true of course that such a step into the blue might have come not simply from courage but from a lack of imagination. The consequences might not have been foreseen. Had he foreseen them himself when he had made his leap northward? What had he been looking for? Was it for a change of scenery or for a challenge in his old age? Was it out of a romantic surmise that what appeared simple was best? For in fact this life was far from simple. That was the mistake made, that the life of the country was simpler than that of the town. On the contrary it was much more complicated, as relations within the family were more intricate than with outsiders. Had he foreseen all the consequences himself, as for instance that his wife might not like the life? Had he himself shown stupidity, not made sufficiently precise calculations so that the rocket that had sprung so quickly from the ground had inched, O so minutely, from its proper trajectory to land at last in a direction not plotted?

"I still think," he repeated, "that it is we who must change."

And what was that girl doing now? He had met her once purely by chance as he was coming home by train and she had sat with him in the same carriage. She was wearing green slacks and a green jacket. All the way she had been reading a woman's magazine, pausing only to light cigarette after cigarette. Once their eyes had happened to meet and at that moment he had been questioned not by a mind but by a body totally aware of its own power, intensely and shamelessly inhabited. Their gazes had dropped away from each other and she had gone back to the magazine while he himself had read his *Guardian* and the carriage became the neutral cage in which the two of them momentarily existed.

"Why don't we invite them here some night?" he said.

"Invite who here?"

"The minister and his wife. They might easily come. And why shouldn't they? After all I am an elder in the church."

"Of course they'll come," said his wife.

"Well then, we will have to give them something to eat, won't we?"

"Naturally," said Martha.

"In that case we'll do that."

Adapt, adapt, or go under. That was the demand that the world made on one continually.

"That's settled then. See how easy it is." And he smiled at her.

If one examined the options then one would come to a decision and that was all that was required of one, and the picture of the girl taking the train so headlong into the city faded like smoke from his mind.

He took out his diary. "What night shall we say then?"

17

EDDIE'S PLACE WAS as untidy and crowded as ever. They were all standing about in a large unfurnished room, the stuff from which had been cleared into the lobby, with the boxes of books, the bin full of rubbish, and clothes, even, flung on the floor. A record player was blaring and there were bottles on the table which was the only piece of furniture in the room apart from a greenish sagging armchair. Terry was talking to a girl who was wearing a long kaftan dress, and holding a bottle of whisky. When he saw her he waved the bottle above his head like a boxer.

"Enjoying yourself?" said Eddie.

She shook her head as if to clear it.

"Yes," she said wanly.

"Fine, fine, that's just fine." She thought that he spoke with a false American accent.

"Have some more. What are you drinking?"

"Gin," she said bravely.

She glanced at her watch. It was one in the morning. She drank rapidly from the glass that he put in her hand.

The record player was switched off and Eddie went to the centre of the room.

"Lorna will now play for us." There was a clapping of hands and the girl with the guitar took up her position in the silence that descended afterwards. She was wearing a lace shawl and a long green dress. She played *Country Roads*. "Mountain mama," she sang in her fake nasal American voice. Chrissie felt sick. She stumbled out into the corridor over the bodies of people who were sitting on the bare wooden floor. She turned right, staggering a little. She pushed open the door of the bathroom and locked it behind her. She leaned over the basin and tried to be sick. Green bile threaded the water like shredded grass. She tried to drag the sickness from her stomach but it wouldn't come. She knelt on the floor in front of the toilet bowl, clasping it with both hands.

She stood and stared at her white face in the mirror. It seemed to her that her head was like a skull. She went back to the toilet bowl again, but couldn't be sick. She thought she was going to die and she was frightened. She drank some water and then staggered back to the room where the girl was still singing.

"West Virginia," she sang, her eyes closed, her voice wavering between her native Glasgow accent and the American one she had heard on television and on records.

Chrissie stood at the door watching. Hump-backed Eddie was leaning against the wall, his head swaying to the music. Terry had his arm around the girl in the kaftan dress. Now and again he would take another swig from the bottle of whisky. Chrissie felt sick again. If she wasn't sick she would die. She turned away from the room and went blindly into the corridor. All around her was a becalmed wreckage of detritus, which however swayed as she swayed. A chair stood in front of her slightly askew and she stared at it owlishly. If she could only sit on it, but she couldn't, for it was among such a lot of boxes and dusty carpets. She opened the main door of the flat and went outside, pulling it behind her. She stood on the landing and leaned on the bannister. She looked down into the spiralling vacancy below her and imagined herself falling and falling, spinning over and over like a doll. Very carefully she made her way down the stair clutching the bannister. It seemed that she had walked for hours when she finally reached the bottom. She walked out of the close and saw along the streets the black bags full of rubbish which the wind was shifting. She walked towards the main street and turned left. She waited. If only a taxi would come. She looked up into the dizzying sky and saw the room where the party was taking place. Shadows moved against the light. She began to gulp fresh air into her lungs. If necessary she would walk. The street itself was deserted but when she raised her head to the sky she could see the moon, a half boat tilted in the sky and below and to the right of it Venus which was burning brightly. She walked on steadily and heard the hollow echo of her heels on the road. But there was no one to be seen, only the street lamps were burning with their sickening yellow light. In the eerie light she could see the tenements rising like vast black cliffs from the road towards the sky.

What was she doing there at one in the morning?

At that moment she felt the sickness rising in her and she bent over and the stuff poured out all over the pavement. She glanced at it dully. It was mixed with fragments of food. She took out a handkerchief and wiped her mouth. Then she stood up slowly, grasping the railings beside her. She staggered on. It seemed to her that the street was rising up against her, that she was sailing into a choppy sea. She thought again that she was going to die. If only there was a place where she could sit down. She walked on and came to a bench. She leaned her head against the cold wood which had drops of dew on it. She closed her eyes and felt she could go to sleep. But then with an effort she opened them and said to herself, No, I can't do that. Where was Terry? He had stayed away from her all night and when she had protested he had said

"What the bloody hell is the point of going to a party unless you meet new people?"

That bitter angry rage had suddenly filled him again and she had been frightened. How little she had really known him! The yellow lights troubled her: it was as if they belonged to an alien country which she hated.

A black cat ran along silently in front of her. A sign of good luck, she thought. If only I could sleep. The black cat turned and she saw its green wedge-shaped eyes. On the other side of the street she saw a drunk staggering along, shouting and swearing to himself.

"There's nae team like the Glasgow Rangers," he was shouting, "no, not one, no, not one." His voice was off key and now and again he would turn and shake his fist at the whole yellow deserted city. His long scarf trailed to the ground.

"No not one, no not one," she heard, and then the words faded into the distance.

There were trees on the other side of the road and a park beyond. She thought that perhaps she would go into the park and sleep but a voice warned her, "You'd better not. You never know who's there." She got up from the bench and came to a bus stop against which she leaned, and then was sick again. She squeezed sickness like toothpaste from the tube of her body. And then as if it were an act of God she saw a taxi approaching. Let its yellow light be on, she prayed, let it be on. Its yellow light was on and she waved it down. She opened the door and slumped into the back seat.

"Bank Street," she said. "Number 19."

Voices gibbered monotonously at the driver and she thought that they were talking to her. She rocked back and forward on the leather seat like a doll. She leaned back and closed her eyes. And all the time the driver stared ahead of him and didn't speak. He didn't even whistle or hum. And all the time the voices gibbered. Now and again amidst the incessant stream of words she would hear an address being given, and then she would slump into the back of the seat again.

Finally the taxi drew to a stop and the taxi driver told her, "A pound and ten pence." She fumbled in her handbag and found the money. He drew away from the kerb and she turned towards her flat. She entered the close and set her feet upward for the climb. Very slowly she made her way up the steps. When she reached the top she took the key out of her bag and fitted it shakily into the lock. Then she dashed into the room and lay spinning on the bed. It seemed to her that she did not recognise the room. She clung to the bed with outspread hands as if she were crucified.

18

"YOU SHOULDN'T WORRY about your son," said Annie to Morag Bheag as the two of them stood together in the village shop. "You should turn your eyes to the East. I'll have some yoghourt, please, Sandy.

"You see," she went on, "the Buddha sat under a tree and revelations came to him. We must be freed from desire for earthly goods, not like Sheena Macnab. I hear she's just bought a new bedroom suite from Littlewoods."

"I don't know," said Morag Bheag from the point of whose nose a drop of water was hanging. "You do worry, whether you like it or not."

"That's right," said Sandy. "Anyone who has a son in Ireland is bound to worry."

He leaned over the counter, waiting for Annie's next order. Of course she was an old woman but there was a streak of brilliance there.

"I will tell you," said Annie. "What you should strive for is the condition of Nirvana. That is, you dissolve into nothingness. You do not care any longer for possessions. Before that of course there are cycles of rebirth. I myself think that in a previous existence I was a professor in Egypt. If you study such subjects you will find that substances have been found that modern science cannot analyse. There were people here from another planet, here, years and years ago. And what about the Bermuda Triangle? All these pilots disappearing. I'll have a plain loaf, I think, Sandy. So my advice to you is not to worry but to try to attain the condition of Nirvana."

Morag Bheag thought miserably, "That's all right for you. You don't have any children."

Sandy brought the loaf over and laid it in front of Annie on the counter. He hoped that the supermarket wouldn't come in the near future, not till he had retired from the business which his father had left him. He could quite see why Morag Bheag should be worried, any sane person would be.

"How long is he going to be in Ireland for?" he asked.

"I think it is six months," said Morag. "I think that is what they do."

"Protestants and Catholics," said Annie with determination. "That is what you get if you believe in Christianity. There is nothing but guns and fighting. It happened before in the Thirty Years' War and there was Joan of Arc whom they burned to death. Confucius wanted everyone to be a gentleman but I don't think that is enough. Was Hitler a gentleman? What you want to be is indifferent to the concerns of life. That is what the Buddha teaches. Of course there are people who said that you should go about naked and eat little food but I don't think that was right. If you study the Pyramids you will find that the king's servants were killed as well as the king: that was to help him in a future life. But in my opinion that was going too far. Royalty was only interested in possessions. Of course they had chariots and they believed in cats. By the way I hear that David Collins' cat was run over yesterday and the driver didn't stop. They shouldn't keep cats here. There is far too much traffic."

"That's right," said Sandy. "Still, I would have thought that it would have known the rules of the road by now. That cat was fourteen years old."

"You do not know the day or the hour," said Annie pointing to the cartons of cottage cream. "I'll have one of those. If we knew the day and the hour and what was going to happen that would be predestination and that wouldn't be good. If you study the great religions you will find that people sat under a tree and thought, and forgot about themselves. That is what we should all do. If a man is sitting under a tree thinking he is not harming his neighbour. I don't think anything will happen to your son, Morag. He is a soldier in this life but perhaps in another life he will be a peacemaker."

"They say they have found metals in Egypt that the scientists don't know anything about," said Sandy.

"Most people here read only the Reader's Digest," said Annie dismissively. "They do not make enough use of the library in the town. There are more things in heaven and earth than we know about. Sandy, your potatoes were poor, the last lot I got. They were very wet and some of them were green. Where did you get them from?"

"The usual. I don't understand why they should be like that."

"I am okay," said Morag remembering the last letter she got: "It's not as bad as people say. I'll be getting some leave at Christmas." How could Annie know anything about children since she hadn't had any children of her own? She was too selfish for that. And how could Sandy know either? You had to be a mother to feel the things that she felt, to remember the things that she remembered. Of course they disobeyed you and you had quarrels but they were still your own flesh and blood.

"Is he sending you money?" said Annie. "You make sure that he sends you money. The officers can deal with that. Otherwise he'll spend all his money on cigarettes and drink. The young people of today don't care about anyone but themselves. Why are we getting so many strikes if that isn't right? We're heading for the Apocalypse. Look at the rate of inflation we're having, and the wars all over the globe. I think that's all, Sandy. And make sure that you add it up right."

Certainly, thought Morag, when George had that job in the garage he wouldn't give her any money and they had a lot of arguments about it. When I was your age, she had said, I gave all my money to my parents. Who do you think is paying for your food, and if you were in lodgings you wouldn't leave your room in that condition.

"I'll tidy my room when I go to the army," he had told her, so impudent and quick.

"You wait," she had told him, "you wait till you are in the army. You'll find it's not all that you think it is. And another thing, you should get as many certificates as you can from the school. You never know when they'll come in handy. You should be studying."

"I don't like school," he had said and turned on the television again. She was tired of that television though they could only afford a black and white.

"That will be one pound eighty-five," said Sandy to her. She took out her purse and counted the money into his hand. What was he doing in Ireland anyway? She had warned him about it. But he would come in and say, "There's a programme about the Army tonight, mum." And then at Christmas he had come in drunk. Of course it wasn't serious but you had to watch them all the time.

She handed over two pounds and waited till she got her change.

"You tell him I was asking for him," said Annie magisterially. "Tell him to turn away from Christianity and look towards the East. Look what they did to Christ, they crucified him. But they didn't crucify the Buddha and even if they had he would have gone into a state of Nirvana and he wouldn't have felt anything. That's the great advantage of Nirvana. Look at what they're saying about the silicon chip. They think they know everything. But what is the silicon chip? Nothing. There are millions of unemployed people in India and they worship the cow. But they have their own reasons for that. Which reminds me, Mrs Berry hasn't sold her calf yet. I was telling her that she should. They're not worth what you pay for them in feeding stuff."

"You're right enough," said Sandy. "Feeding stuff is very expensive these days."

Morag Bheag prepared to leave. Nothing that Annie had said had made her worry less about George. Every morning at seven o'clock she put on the news to hear what was happening in Ireland.

"Now," said Annie, "I will tell you about David Collins' cat. Three things will happen. These things always come in threes. You mark my words. The same thing happened when I lost the sheep. Angus Berry was the next to go and after that it was Elizabeth's mother. If you study the Eastern religions you don't think about things like that. You're indifferent to these things."

"We should all sit under trees," Morag Bheag thought laughingly to herself. "Just like dogs." There were plenty of trees around the village. Maybe Annie should sit under one eating yoghourt.

She said cheerio and left the shop looking small and dispirited.

"That woman," said Annie, "worries too much. There is no use in that. Sufficient unto the day is the evil thereof. I hear the minister's wife's planning an open air party, the day of the Sunday School picnic. I shall certainly be there."

"I'm afraid," said Sandy diplomatically, "that I don't know anything about that. Anyway I can't leave the shop."

"Huh," said Annie. "Remember this, Sandy, you can't take it with you. There are no pockets in a shroud, as the saying goes."

And she left the shop walking with her usual slanted urgent gait as if she were heading into a high wind. Sandy looked after her affectionately. One thing you could say for her, she was a good crack.

19

KENNY FOOLISH SAT in front of the house, his head bent over a piece of wood which he was carving into the semblance of a duck, just like the one Mrs Berry had. Alisdair and Hugh approached him coming from opposite directions. He smiled at them radiantly but didn't speak.

"Did you see the Jap?" said Hugh. "There's a Jap in our house." And he pressed an imaginary trigger making the sound of a machine-gun. There was a programme on TV about them. They had attacked Pearl Harbor.

"The 'planes were lying on the ground," said Alisdair. "They were cheats." Kenny Foolish didn't say anything. The duck grew more clearly under his hand. He was chewing a piece of grass which hung from the side of his mouth. The sun was warm on his hands and on his face. He was happy. He saw the brown train chugging gently along the track.

The two boys gazed tenderly at the duck. Everyone knew that Kenny wasn't all there of course. They should keep away from him, their parents had said. Kenny Foolish raised his head from the duck and smiled. He smelt the roses and the rank grass and he felt the knife in his hand. There was a contented hum around him.

"They starved the prisoners of war," said Alisdair. "The little girl eats chocolates. She's very small."

Kenny Foolish looked ahead of him and saw the water sparkling in the sun. The duck's head took shape. He liked the warmth and the humming. He liked the flowers some of which were like small yellow suns.

"My mum said David Collins' cat went to heaven," said Hugh.

"That's right," said Alisdair. "He's with God in heaven."

"Why do you think he's in heaven, Kenny?" said Hugh. "Do you think God has mice?"

Kenny smiled his radiant smile. The head wasn't right. It was too . . . he couldn't think what it was too.

"I think," said Alisdair, "that God wanted the cat for himself. Maybe Mr Collins should get a dog now."

The completed duck lay in Kenny's hand. It was wooden and perfectly shaped. The two boys looked at it and in turn touched it. It seemed as if it was ready to fly. Kenny watched them and the duck and he was happy. The knife in his hand glittered like a fish from the river.

The heat of the sun was on the back of his hand.

20

THE REVEREND PETER MURCHISON and Mr Scott sat in the latter's living-room while the two ladies were in the kitchen.

"Would you care for a sherry?" said Mr Scott, opening a cupboard above which there was a painting of what appeared to be a green fawn in a wood.

"I wouldn't say no," said the minister.

After the meal he felt full and almost in a mood for confession.

"What would you say," he said, "about a person, a Christian, who had lost his or her faith?"

"Are you talking about Annie?" said Mr Scott, smiling. "I hear she's gone all Eastern."

"No, I wasn't thinking of her," said the minister slowly, glancing at the obligatory television set, the long red curtains, the bookcase.

"Is there someone else then?" said Scott, placing a glass of sherry on a small table in front of the minister.

"There is," said the minister decisively. Scott looked at him keenly, then turned away and sat on the sofa.

"I don't know what to do," said the minister. "This man used to believe implicitly in God. His whole life radiated from that belief, and now he no longer has any."

"And why did he lose his belief," said Mr Scott, gazing at him with sharp shrewd eyes.

"He doesn't know, that's the whole point of the story," said the minister slowly. He doesn't know. Do you think faith can come and go?"

"It's not for me to say," said Scott. "I can't say that I've ever had that sort of belief. My whole life hasn't been run on belief. Of course I believe but I have never examined my belief. Belief for me fits the facts."

"Yes, this man thought that too," said the minister reflectively. "But now he doesn't believe that that is the case. He says that his life is like a continual tiredness. In the beginning he would set out in the morning as if he were a missionary. Now everything feels heavy and old. What do you think of that?"

"Well," said Scott, "when I came to this village at first I felt the same. I was sure I had made a mistake. There were so many people that I didn't know, and at first they wouldn't have anything to do with us. I felt they resented us."

"But you don't feel like that now," said the minister, leaning forward eagerly. "I mean you have done a lot of good work here. You and your wife are on so many committees. Surely you don't feel like that now."

Scott put his glass down slowly on the table and said, "It's difficult to tell. Sometimes I wake up in the morning and I feel as if I'm in the wrong place. I don't seem to fit, to mesh with my surroundings. It's very difficult to explain. Then the day passes and I'm all right again. There is something missing that I regret. Can you understand that? It's as if I'd left a part of myself behind. The only reason that we came here to live permanently was because we used to come on holiday here and we liked the place. But being on holiday in a place and living in it are two different things."

"Yes, I can see that," said the minister with the same eagerness. "It's as if the repetitiveness of the world gets us down. I wonder sometimes whether too much examination of the world is good for one." He sipped his sherry. "It's as if we . . ." He stopped and continued again. "Some people accept the work of the seasons and the day and do not wish to see beyond that." His voiced trailed off.

"I think I see what you are getting at," said Mr Scott. "I used to feel the same about the bank. And yet routine is surely our salvation. Surely?"

"I quite see that," said the minister, his face pale and intent. "I quite see it. It's only that I feel we should get a bonus of grace now and again, like interest in the bank. You see, I'm an intellectual being. It's in my nature. Yet the significance of the world as it says in the Bible can be revealed even to little children. The mind has nothing to do with it. Christ entered the world vertically from above but the horizontal world is our province. I can understand that. He entered history and transformed it. The thing about Him is His continual radiance and freshness. It must have been a place like this

90

that he came to: his language surprises us by its radiance. How can we tap his power at its source, its simplicity? I feel as if the answer is all very simple, like drinking water, like seeing a stone in its uncorrupted nature without the shine of human beings on it. Prayer, I've prayed." He had given up all pretence now and was talking as if the putative man who had lost his faith was in fact himself, as indeed he was.

"To live well and with simplicity, how difficult it is."

"Yes," said Scott slowly, looking at him with compassion. "Yes, there ought to be a way of living like that. And yet, aren't you romanticising? Aren't you idealising the children?"

"Oh, I know that," said the minister impatiently. "I have children of my own. They were jealous of each other. They fought each other all the time. They were not innocent. And yet they had the capacity to surprise. Do you see? They had the capacity to see the world in a new way. Listen, some time ago I was reading about Einstein. What happened to him? He had no facts other than those which were already provided. But he looked at them as if they were new. So instead of saying a train leaves a station at forty miles an hour he says that the station leaves the train at forty miles an hour. And both are right. Yet only he had the childlike mind to see it. I look out every day from my window at the rails. They are heading somewhere, the train is constrained by them. The question is how to get off the rails and remain true and loyal and faithful and astonished. If there is one woman in the village I admire it is Mrs Berry. She has strength. Where does she get it from? She is never afraid and the world never becomes stale for her. Do you understand what I'm saying?" He wiped the sweat from his brow with a handkerchief.

"I think so," said Scott. "When I retired from my work I felt the same. I felt disoriented. I would wander about the house like a ghost, picking something up and then putting it down again. That was why I left England, I know that now. I wanted as it were a second chance. It must have been as you say. The world needed a second chance, and got it through Christ."

"Yes, yes," said the minister with the same glowing eagerness. "That is what I'm talking about, a second chance. You know the way you are typing something and you are using carbon and it seems wrinkled and old and used. You want to throw it away. It's as if we want to throw the first life away and have a new one. How did you cope?" he asked abruptly.

"How did I cope," said Scott meditatively. "It's difficult to say. It's a question of letting the springs of action run down. Of realising that one must accept what there is, taking pleasure in small things if one can." He smiled suddenly. "I grew interested in gossip again. In the doings of ordinary people like myself. And then very slowly the world accommodated itself to me. That is what happened."

"Yes," said the minister, "but I don't want that. I want the world to be as glorious as it once was, to be as radiant. When I came here first I didn't think there was a place as beautiful as this in the world. I had come from the city, you understand, and then one summer I came here and it seemed to me it was like heaven. Every shadow cast by every stone was clear, almost solid. The hedges seemed to blossom with words. You cannot imagine what it was like. Things . . ." he tried to grasp it, "Things . . . they were like . . . Listen, have you ever seen that visual trick where you stare at a certain shape for a long time and then you turn from it and you look at a blank wall and as you do so an after-image forms itself? I saw one once and do you know that the after-image was the face of Christ. It hovered in front of me. I would look at the floor and then raise my eyes again and the image persisted. It was as if the image of Christ was with me all the time. Do you understand? But I don't feel that now."

"Can any of us," said Scott gently. "Are you asking too much? After all we grow old and we are none of us perhaps privileged."

"But I want it to be like that," said the minister fiercely. "I do not want faith to grow tired. Is it perhaps that it is not sufficiently tested here? In this calm place? Is that what it is?"

"I don't know," said Scott. They gazed at each other in a common union of despair and yet of hope. Eventually the silence was broken when the minister said, "I think I hear the ladies coming. They must have finished the dishes."

As if in a secret conspiracy they smiled at each other and Scott said, "Yes I can hear them. My wife will have been showing yours the house. She always does that."

"Mary does the same," said the minister smiling affectionately. For some reason there came into his mind the phrase, "In my father's house there are many mansions," and he felt utterly exhausted as if the words, bare and uncalled for, had reminded him of a world that he could no longer enter.

The two of them rose to their feet as their wives came in.

"Discussing theology no doubt," said Mrs Scott, and Mary smiled. Even my love for you is not enough, thought the minister, even that is not enough.

21

MURDO MACFARLANE WALKED heavily into the small garden at the back of his house. He dug in the soil with his graip and took out the potatoes, shaking them free of dirt. He put about a dozen of them into a small blue bucket that he had carried with him from the kitchen. As he was doing this he was aware on the rim of his sight of the other plot where he had his turnips and his carrots. Some day he thought that perhaps he would plant parsley and maybe have a hothouse for those striped tomatoes that had once been given him by George Miller who raised them and gave some to the villagers. As he bent down he felt his knees creaking and his sight blurring a little but he knew that it wasn't anything serious. Carrying the bucket in his hand he walked past the tool-shed where he kept among other things his hammer and chisel and nails and an old churn that his mother had used when she was making cheese. Automatically and without thinking he checked that the padlock was on the door and that none of these vandals had been trying to get in. Before he entered his house by the back door he shook his shoes free of the dirt that they had accumulated, and watched for a moment the hens moving about in their black skirts like old women taking the air.

He went into the combined kitchen and scullery, shutting the door behind him. He went over to the sink and put the potatoes in a yellow plastic basin, and then washed them. He frowned slightly: he had been meaning to buy two of those rubber things that you could fit on the taps so that you could spray the water in any direction. He scraped the potatoes and turned the tap off. He poured out the dirty water from the basin and refilled it with fresh water and washed the potatoes again. Bending down he took a pan from the cupboard below the sink and put the potatoes in it and ran water over them. He placed the pan on the nearest ring of the cooker, for he had discovered that the inner ring didn't work too well. He took the salt container down from on top of the cooker and poured some salt into the pan then switched the cooker on.

After he had done that he went to the cupboard and set the table with one blue plate, a knife and fork, a cup which was bitten at the edges, sugar, butter, milk, and two biscuits which he took from a tin which he kept in a drawer. Then from the bottom part of the cupboard he took a tin of ham, opened it with the tin opener and put some of it on the plate. The rest he removed from the tin and placed on another plate which he coverd with a pudding dish.

Then he sat down on a chair and began to read the *Express*. But before he could start he noticed that there were spots of dirt on the linoleumed floor and he began to clean it with a brush, putting the dirt on a shovel which he then tilted into the bin. He put the brush back in the corner and began to read. He didn't read about the Afghanistan invasion but looked for small paragraphs about people. One paragraph told him about a father who had snatched his little daughter from her mother at gun point. He read very carefully, making little movements with his mouth, and moving his neck all the time as if his collar was too tight for him. He didn't miss one single word and took perhaps seven minutes to read the story. After he had finished the first story he read a second one which told him about a beauty queen who had run away with a new boyfriend leaving her husband behind. The husband wanted her back and had said, according to the reporter, "I will forgive her anything." While he was reading, the potatoes began to boil and the light shining through the window made big panes on the floor. He heard a hissing sound and went over and turned down the switch for the ring on which the potatoes were boiling. When the water was bubbling merrily but not spilling over he sat down again in his chair. "Climber saved by fingertips," he read. He moved steadily from word to word, sometimes returning to one if the sentence didn't seem to make sense. He twisted his neck and his lips moved and the water in the pan bubbled.

After a while he went over and tested the potatoes with a fork to see if they were ready. He frowned because he had allowed them to become too soft. Then holding the lid of the pan at a slant he poured the hot water down the sink and placed the pan on the ring again, turning the heat down. After the potatoes were dry he placed them on the plate beside the cold ham that he had taken from the tin. Then he sat down and began to eat, chewing carefully and with relish, and when he had finished he placed the plate in the sink. Then he boiled the water in the kettle and made his tea, using one tea-bag only. In order to make the tea stronger he stirred the bag with a spoon, then he poured the tea into a cup, buttered bread, and ate it with his tea. When he had finished his tea he put the milk, sugar, and butter and bread into the cupboard noticing that there was a slice of plain loaf still in the breadpan with green mould on it. He took it out and put it in the bin. Then he washed the knife, cup, fork and spoon, hung the cup on a hook, and put the cutlery in a drawer. He returned to his chair and read some more of the *Express*, now and again looking up to see if any bird had entered his bird house. One had. It was a blue tit, a beautiful bird which haunted his garden every summer.

Later on he would go to the shop. In the evening he might watch the television or visit David Collins. For his tea he would have beans with the remainder of the ham and perhaps some of that fresh butter that Sandy sold in his shop. His mouth watered when he thought of its creamy taste. Till then he might do some work in the garden but before that he would have a snooze in his chair. He closed his eyes after placing the *Express* over his face and prepared to sleep. As he did so he began to think of the girl Elizabeth who came to help David Collins. Why did she hardly ever visit him? Was there something wrong with him? Though he had only one eye he wasn't a monster. From thinking of Elizabeth his thoughts moved to his mother whose bones were mouldering in the churchyard. He never put any flowers on her grave, and he knew that people talked about that. She would now be a tangle of bones anyway. He was walking through summer with the postbag on his shoulders. A stoat suddenly ran across the road in front of him, stopping to gaze at him with cloudless shining penetrating eyes and then eeling its way through a hole in the wall. He knocked on a door and it opened. "A parcel for you," he said. The woman who was wearing an almost transparent nightdress invited him in. She said, "I have always loved you. You are the best postman there has ever been. I love your conscience." He put the bag down. She floated ahead of him, turning to look with untroubled yet inviting eyes. He slept, smiling. Now and again he passed his hand unconsciously over his face as if brushing away a fly.

22

"ARE YOU SURE you want to get rid of all the paperbacks?" said the minister's wife to her husband.

"I'm quite sure." He was sitting in the green armchair, the *Scotsman* in front of him, spectacles down on his nose.

"A hundred books you want to get rid of. Why, that's all you have," she went on. There was something here that she didn't understand.

"Yes," said the minister calmly. "I want to get rid of them. You can put them in boxes and I'll put them in the boot of the car. Mrs Berry's daughter is running a bookstall, I think you said."

"But look," she insisted. "These are good books. They are religious books."

"Yes," said the minister patiently, putting down his paper. "They are by Barth and Niebuhr and Kierkegaard. And I'm finished with them." He was really finished with them, he wanted to give them away, there must be someone else who might want to read them, they hadn't helped him at all. What use was academic information to a minister when at the end his job was to be at the bedside of a dying man, reading the service for the bride in her white dress, comforting the sick.

"Yes," he said with finality, "I'm finished with them."

For some reason she shivered as if a dark shade had crossed the sun, as if there was standing at the door with a telegram in his hand a man not with a head but a skull. She often had these premonitions and she couldn't explain their origin to herself.

"Have you weighed yourself recently," she said, "I think you've lost weight."

"I'm all right," said the minister. "You just give them the paperbacks. Maybe Annie will buy them though there are none about the East."

But the frown on her face persisted. He didn't like that knitting of her forehead, the twisted paths that were like the tracks left by snails.

"Sometimes I'm worried about you," she said. Her one quarrel with him was his secretiveness, his silent endurance, his keeping from her the pain he suffered. She knew that he thought more deeply than she did, that in fact she herself lived in the world's continual traffic, that when it came to changing a nappy for instance he was useless. And yet her two sons had respected him for he hadn't been at all bigoted with them. Truly she hadn't missed the money that other people made. Now and again of course since human nature was human nature she would look at catalogues and think, I would like that ring or that potato peeler or that new hoover. But she had learned not to love possessions, for her husband was totally indifferent to them, his mind was bare and simple. Indeed if it weren't for her he would walk about the place with his shirt hanging out of his trousers and his face unshaven. He was like a saint: that was the only word that could describe him.

In all the time he had been in the village he had never asked anything for himself, he bore implied insults with good humour, as if he didn't belong to the world that ordinary people inhabited.

He had turned back to the *Scotsman* and something in the way he held it in front of him brought her terror back again. It was as if a crack had opened in the sky and she sensed a crumbling and breaking, steady, silent and persistent. I should put my arms around him and hold him close, but he doesn't like these demonstrations of affection, they embarrass him. Of course he was brighter than her, he had been the best student of his year at Theological College, but in a deep sense he was still a child. She dreaded what would happen if she died before him, he would be lost in the world. And she knew that he wouldn't want to stay with his children however much he liked them.

You have done well, you good and faithful servant, she thought in silent tribute. And yet, and yet, there was something. He had lost weight. She who never bothered about her weight though it was women's perpetual topic was frightened now. They had once been young and they had gazed into each other's eyes in cafes in the city, had climbed the Mound to see round the old historic castle, and yet the faces that they now presented to the world seemed to be much the same, immortal in love. They had grown old in reciprocal tune with each other. Time was an eternal miracle. But something had changed. It was like a bell striking, a small metal bell.

"Are you sure you're all right?" she said. "You're perfectly sure?"

"Perfectly," he said, without raising his eyes from the *Scotsman*. "There's nothing wrong with me. And you can take the books and sell them all. I have plenty more books, enough to keep me going. Anyway it will give you more space. You can always put dishes in the cupboards from which you take the books."

"It's not that," she said. "I was not thinking about that. I was thinking about you."

"For the last time," he replied. "I'm all right. And for the last time you can take the books with no guilt complex."

"All right then, dear. If you're sure you'll be all right." She almost bit her tongue off. "I'll run down with them now."

"You do that, dear," he said. "Now go away and leave me to read the letter page of the *Scotsman*. I hadn't realised there were so many teachers in the world."

She went out of the room to hunt for cardboard boxes. "Look, girl," she told herself firmly. "You take yourself in hand. Just get the cardboard boxes, put the books in them and take them down to Mrs Berry's daughter. That is what you have to do." Sometimes her husband would call her Martha. "You are the dearest one," he would say, "the one who keeps the world going. The one with the flour on her hands and face." And he had once shown her a painting of a woman with big red arms and a big bosom pouring milk from a red jug into a red ewer. "Thank you," he had said, "thank you." She bent down to pack the books in the cardboard boxes which she had found in the attic among her children's discarded toys.

23

THE STATION CLOCK said 6.05 when Chrissie Murray passed through the barrier showing her ticket to the grimily dressed ticket collector. She looked at the queue that was forming at platform seven but didn't recognise anyone. Her stomach was churning over and over and all she wanted was to sit in a corner of a carriage by herself, or hide behind the newspaper she had bought for that purpose. At 6.15 the train drew in and she made for a corner seat in a non-smoker. Immediately she sat down she put the newspaper in front of her face and pretended to read. Now and again from behind the newspaper she would see young men and girls with kitbags over their shoulders struggling along the corridor, hikers who would probably leave the train at Crianlarich. At 6.18 the train drew out of the station, rocking at first from side to side as if not quite sure whether it should go or not, and then finally settling down to a smooth rhythm. From behind the shelter of the newspaper she looked through the window at the cans and cartons and fragments of paper strewn along the track, at the slogans advertising gangs drawn in red war-paint on walls, at the evening sun that glanced off the rails. She felt numb and dull and the taste of lipstick was salt on her lips.

The train picked up speed and the stations passed in a blur. Sometimes she saw council houses uniformly standing beside each other and, once, a fire as if someone was burning rubbish. The train's motion generated in her mind words which said 'Going Home, Going Home.' She rested her head on the dirty white cloth behind her and shut her eyes but when she did so she seemed to see Terry's face as he prepared to go to work that morning. She opened her eyes again and found that the train had stopped at Dumbarton. There, too, she saw the big gang slogans scrawled, the names immortalised here if nowhere else. The Gents had been boarded up and the bookstall was shut. What have I done? she asked herself. Am I a shuttlecock to move from place to place? The train started to move and again she closed her eyes.

Later she opened them again, for as they passed Dumbarton she saw cows grazing in a field in the evening light. They raised their heads as the train passed and then bent down again and began to graze. Now she saw water to the left of her and ships in a bay. The ships were big and grey and the water smooth and red with the light of the sun. Once she saw a large ship with a name on it that she couldn't make out: perhaps it was Russian or Dutch. I could jump out, she thought, if only I had the nerve. And she was seized by panic as she thought of her return. For the next weeks, months, she would have to live with what she had done. Chrissie Murray, they would say years hence, of course she was the one who ran away and then came back. She would carry that stigma with her forever.

The train was steadily climbing now and she could see the moors on her right hand side. Strangely enough in spite of her panic, she was beginning to feel more at home, as if some deep need in her nature were responding to those lands through which she was now passing. The fear was still there like the surface disturbance on water, but, below, the current was moving with confidence. Once she put her head out of the window and saw behind her the long curving rear of the train as if it were a snake winding in and out of the landscape. She hoped that it would be dark when she arrived home so that she might be able to walk from the station without anyone seeing her, pass through the gate in the field and rush into the safety of her house. If he didn't want her back that would be the end, and she winced as if the thought were unbearable.

There came into her mind without thinking about it the story of the Prodigal Son that the minister had once told the class in Sunday School. The Prodigal Son had left his house because he didn't want to work on the land and he had found everything around him boring. He had left, she imagined, on a fine spring day when the whole world was sparkling and then he had found himself derelict, feeding on the stuff that the pigs ate. She saw him crouched among the big grey stranded pigs which were like grey ships in the dung. She saw him sitting in a hovel, brooding. Then she saw him making a decisive movement and setting off home. He was carrying a stick and he was walking along an autumn road while the acorns fell from the oaks, landing on the ground. She saw him approaching his house. His father and his older brother were both working in the field picking potatoes. At first his father didn't know him for he looked like a tramp and the sun was in his father's eyes. Then his father ran towards him and gathered him in his arms. The minister's face was shining with triumph. Welcome to the one sinner who had returned, he was saying, and his pale face glowed. And in the field the older son was still standing, resting his arms on the spade, angry and bitter.

She glanced through the window. The train was approaching Crianlarich where it usually stopped for ten minutes or so. She saw the passengers leaving their carriages and reappearing with sausage rolls and cups of tea from the restaurant. She stayed where she was for she couldn't have eaten anything. Again she searched the faces to see if there was anyone she knew but there was no one. After a while the train moved again, and in a strange way she knew that she was going home. It wasn't anything that she could put into words. The feeling must have emanated from the familiarity of the landscape but she knew that it was deeper than that. In spite of her fear she felt a rightness in the place where she was. Along the road which ran parallel to the railway track she saw a tinker and his wife and children sitting in a cart.

Soon she would have to face what she would have to face. Soon she would have to get out at the station, hand over her ticket to Alex, and soon he would have told everyone that she had returned. Soon she would have to look at familiar faces and behind those faces there would be the thought, "She tried to live in the city but she failed." She knew that they would feel joy at her failure, that her return would justify them in the way of life that they had chosen. Nevertheless she would have to go through with it, there was no alternative. Because she was who she was there was no other choice. She raised the paper in front of her face as a woman passed along the corridor in the direction of the toilet.

The train toiled on. She could see the moors now on both sides of her. Now and again she would catch a glimpse of a loch shining in the sun which was setting beyond the hills. Day after day when she had been washing dishes at home she could see ahead of her the mountain with its engraved trenches through which in the spring the rivers poured joyously. It seemed to be beckoning to her and saying, 'Why don't you take a chance?' And she had taken her chance and failed. Terry hadn't been after all the sort of person she had thought he had been. In the village he had appeared adventurous and animated and new, but in the city he had been as overwhelmed as everybody was. In the city he was nothing, he was a small man who lived in perpetual hope of a future that he would have to work for. Why, even taxi drivers talked contemptuously to him as if he were instantly transparent to them. And who were his friends? Drifters like himself. A hunchback who read space fiction and undressed her with his eyes. The untidiness of the flats she had seen appalled her. How could they live like that as if in the wake of a storm? She saw again in her mind's eye the corridor filled with cardboard boxes of books, the bedroom into which she had strayed and on the floor of which her feet left footprints. She saw the lamp that didn't work, the dusty papers.

Chug chug went the train, a brown worm travelling through the landscape. She put the newspaper down in her lap, having read none of it. She felt as if all that was happening had been fated. Even now she could go to the door and jump and that would be the end of it all. There would be no laughing mocking eyes to outstare. "West Virginia," she thought, "Mountain mama, take me home." The sun had now set and the dusk had fallen. At such a time in the village the birds would be faintly chirping and peace would descend over the earth. At such a time she and John would draw the curtains and watch TV and she would listen to the same words spoken over and over, "Did anything happen today?"

"No, nothing special." At such a time the children would be sleeping in their beds.

Another half hour and she would be arriving at the station. She closed the buttons of her coat as if she were preparing for a meeting or a battle. She rose and went to the toilet. There she stood in front of the mirror swaying with the train, planting her feet firmly as if on a shifting deck, putting lipstick on her lips, and rouge on her pale cheeks. Then she adjusted the green scarf at her throat and returned to her seat. As she looked through the window she could see in the glass the face of a man who sat in the seat across from her and who was reading a paper. As if conscious of her stare he turned and looked at her and smiled. She noticed that one of his cheeks was red as if it had been burned, though it was probably a birthmark. She continued to stare out of the window. Chug chug went the train. She saw the petrol station flashing past, a cottage with lights in it, the river.

It wouldn't be long now. She stood up and took her small case down from the rack, and went to the door. Soon she would have to pull down the window, put her hand on the handle and open the door. She did pull the window down and saw the smoke curling away behind the train. She felt sick and hollow as the decisive moment approached. She felt the train slowing down from its headlong flight and then it had stopped at the station, steam gushing gently from it like white flowers. Case in hand she stepped down when it stopped. Thank God Alex was at the other end of the platform, his back towards her. She rushed past the office and turned right towards Mrs Berry's house in the half darkness. In the dusk she could see the calf to her right in the darkening field. She climbed the brae by the side of the house and then on an impulse and without quite knowing why she was doing it she turned off the path and knocked at Mrs Berry's door.

Mrs Berry was preparing to go to bed when she heard the doorbell ring. She had even taken her teeth out. Quickly she put them back in and prepared to answer the door. Who could it be at this time of night? Most of her visitors came during the day. Maybe she could draw the curtains and see who was there. But on the other hand that might look unmannerly if whoever was standing there saw her. She drew herself upright, turned the key in the lock, and at first didn't recognise the girl; partly because she was the very last person she expected to see at the door at ten o'clock at night.

"It's me, Mrs Berry. It's me. Chrissie Murray."

What was this? Her mind grappled with this strange fact. Chrissie Murray had run away to Glasgow. What was she doing here?

For a moment she trembled as if she were seeing a ghost. Of course ghosts might appear to one. There were stories connected with the islands, and even with the village, though she had never seen one herself.

"May I come in, Mrs Berry?" and she pulled the door wide open and there indeed was Chrissie Murray, exhausted, a small case in her hand. So she had come back after all.

"Come in, come in," she said. "I'll make a cup of tea. You just sit in the kitchen and I'll make a cup of tea." She opened the kitchen door, switched on the light, and looked at the girl who was almost crying. How she had changed: surely she was much thinner. It was as if all the life had gone out of her. So once had Jessie MacCallum looked when she had done the very same thing. Only she hadn't been married when she ran away: how many years ago was that now? She was married in England somewhere. They all thought it was the end of the world. Suddenly without thinking she put her arms around the girl, feeling, as she did so, Chrissie's body trembling.

"There, there, everything's all right," she said. "Everything will be all right. Everything will be all right."

Her mind began to move with a power and precision that astonished herself. Of course the girl would have tea and then she would 'phone her husband. That was the most sensible thing. But the girl was still trembling in her arms as if she were cold.

"There, there, there," she said patting her long hair. "There, there, I'll tell you what. I'm an old biddy now and maybe you could help me with the tea."

Chrissie couldn't understand why she had come to see Mrs Berry. After all it was well known that Mrs Berry disapproved of her parents who had given Chrissie too much money. But she was straight and had told Chrissie's parents that directly to their faces. When Mrs Berry put the kettle on, Chrissie opened the door of the cupboard and took out some biscuits that she found there. Mrs Berry sat at the end of the long table looking at her. There was a long silence. It was as if each was thinking of something that she might say and then dismissing it because it was too raw and insensitive. Finally Mrs Berry said, "When you're as old as I am, lassie, you will know that these things don't matter much. There will be something new next week and then it will all be in the past. I know that John will want you back though it will be hard. Were there many on the train?"

"No," said Chrissie, "there weren't many."

"They always wave to me when I am standing at the window, in the morning and at night." And she paused. "Did you know that Lachlan was going about with other women when he was younger."

"I didn't know that," said Chrissie.

"Of course he was. There's a beam in your own eye as well as in your neighbour's," she added confusedly. "Judge not that ye be not judged." She poured the water into the teapot while she was speaking, while Chrissie stared down dully at the oilcloth on the table.

"My dear," she went on, "did you know that there was a man who lived here who tried to kill his wife? He was one of the upper class as you might say, but I've never met any of them yet that I wouldn't look straight in the eye and say to him, your boots, sir, are on the same earth as me." And her face suddenly flushed and she banged her hand on the table. "And there was another woman here who ran away with her sister's husband. There is no one who doesn't have a secret. I have secrets myself. Did you know that when I was working in the hospital a black man asked me to marry him? Not that I've anything against the blacks for we're all equal in the sight of God but I told him that I wasn't going to India. He made out that he was some kind of prince. But I was too long in the tooth for that." She poured the tea into the two cups and said, "In a short time it'll all be forgotten, lassie. You remember that. There's not one of us that hasn't got a skeleton in his cupboard. There's David Collins there. When he was young he ran away from the shepherding and his father had to go and drag him back. I can still see him holding Davy by the hair and telling him, 'You'll watch these sheep if it's the last thing you do.' No, no, there's secrets everywhere. Is the tea hot enough?"

"Yes, Mrs Berry." How thin and pale the girl looked as if the spirit had gone out of her. Maybe she should have given her some whisky.

"I'll tell you something, Chrissie. You stand up to the whole lot of them. There's not a one of them that's better than yourself. You think of it like that. There's a few I've seen in my time who spent on drink and cigarettes the money that they should have spent on their own children. The cock crows when he's standing among the dung. You remember that. And take your tea."

Chrissie drank her tea slowly and then when she had finished Mrs Berry said, "What you have to do now is 'phone John. There's the 'phone there. Pull the door shut behind you. He's got the car. He'll come and get you."

When Chrissie was at the 'phone she sat at the kitchen table staring ahead of her. How much she would herself give to see Angus coming in that door now, saying, "Well, that's enough of these damned potatoes for today." How much would she not give to see him sitting where that girl had been sitting eating the meat that she had cooked for him. How much for that matter would she not give to be cycling through Edinburgh once more or listening to that matron telling them all off for sneaking in late at night while she herself was meeting someone in the garden. How much would she not give to be on that island again, listening to the first cry of a child, and seeing the mother's face sweaty and yet triumphant. Even yet she had the notebook in which she had taken down her medical notes and sometimes now and again she would glance through it.

Suddenly the door burst open and Chrissie was in the kitchen. "He says it's all right," she shouted joyfully. "He says it's all right. I can go back." And she ran and put her arms around Mrs Berry and kissed her. "I'm so happy." And just as she said this Chrissie felt inside her the little mocking devil who was saying, "This is not a success. This is a failure. You will have to stay here forever." But nevertheless she felt at home again even though she would have to earn it step by step of the way. How old Mrs Berry was looking. Suddenly her face had looked curdled like milk. "Would you like a hot cup of tea?" said Chrissie. "I'm keeping you from your bed."

"No, no, lassie," said Mrs Berry, "you're not keeping me from bed at all. I'll wait till John comes and then he can take you home. You were right to come back. We all make mistakes. Never forget we all have to face up to our mistakes and when you're as old as I am these things don't look so important after all."

They gazed at each other in the silence, listening for the sound of the car. The light blazed around them with a pitiless glare and on the table lay the two cups. Mrs Berry seemed to be holding herself steady by sheer force of will. They heard a car and then it passed into the distance. Then another one and it too faded away. And then at last they saw strong lights at the window and they heard the sound of tyres on gravel.

"I'll be seeing you later," said Mrs Berry. "Don't forget to come in if you feel low." Chrissie kissed her and then ran out into the corridor and then out through the door. Mrs Berry heard her own door shutting and then a car door banging. After a while she heard the car travelling over the gravel again. She rose from the table, took out her teeth and prepared for bed.

107

24

"Apparently," said his wife to the minister, "Kenny Foolish met this Jap on the road the other day and they stood staring at each other. The Jap was trying to find out when the buses went into town and he was speaking in broken English and Kenny Foolish took a fancy to his camera. All Japs seem to have cameras for some reason. Kenny was making signs that he wanted to see the camera and he made a movement towards it. And the Jap thought he was going to attack him. At least that's what Patricia says. It was apparently quite hilarious, Kenny smiling at the Jap and the Jap backing away and Kenny trying to seize the camera. And the Jap was babbling something and Kenny was babbling something else. And eventually the Jap went into the house and told Calum's wife a story about a maniac who was trying to hit him. Meanwhile Kenny was being told by Mr Drummond who happened to be passing that he shouldn't do things like that. Of course Kenny had never seen a Jap before in his life and he called him the Yellow Man. He was quite offended that the Yellow Man shouldn't have let him see what was in the box. Meanwhile it took Calum's wife a long time to explain to the Jap that he hadn't been attacked at all. He kept saying something about the smiling fellow who had tried to hit him."

"It must have been very amusing," said the minister.

"Calum's wife says the Jap is very polite. He eats everything that she gives him though she sometimes thinks that he doesn't like it. His wife and child are just as polite and as tiny as he is. Their English, though, isn't very good. He's some sort of engineer, and his name is Nakamura. The wife and child are like dolls, Calum's wife says."

"Maybe Annie should talk to him. She should ask him about the East. Do you know what she's on about now? I met her and she immediately told me that she was reading an encyclopædia which she saw in the library and it says that there was a sect called the Jains who held that time was divided into immensely long eras and that in each era there were twenty-four perfect beings who appeared on earth. Did I think that these were connected with the twenty-four elders mentioned in Revelations? I nearly told her that it was more probably connected with the number of hours on a twenty-four hour clock. But I didn't say anything. And she sniffed and went away. She thinks I'm a perfect ignoramus."

"Yes, she's always in the library," said Mary. "She spends a lot of her time reading."

While they were talking there was a ring at the doorbell and the minister said, "I wonder who that is at this time of the morning."

"I'll go and see," said his wife.

In a short time she came back with Chrissie Murray. The minister immediately rose from his seat and said, "This is a pleasant surprise. How are you?"

"I'm fine," said the girl. He noticed that she was wearing a longer skirt than usual and that she had got rid of her red boots. Her face was composed and pale. Her hair had been tied at the back into a bun, giving her an almost matronly appearance. His wife was making frantic signs at him behind the girl but he couldn't understand what she was trying to communicate.

"Is there something particular?" he said. "We're so glad to see you again. How is John?"

"John's fine," said the girl who was standing in an embarrassed manner as if there was something she wished to say but couldn't bring herself to do so. His wife's signals were becoming more and more frantic but he couldn't make out what word she was trying to articulate.

"Good, good," said the minister. "Mary, why don't we offer Mrs Murray a coffee?"

"No, no, it's too early," said the girl. "I came because . . ."

His wife's contortions were now manic in their intensity as if she were some kind of idiot making gestures which were completely unintelligible to him. And then at last he remembered.

"Oh, the . . ." He stopped himself in time. "Oh, yes, there was something, Mrs Murray. Some boys found a ring near the railway line. They brought it to me and it was thought at the time that it might be yours. You must have mislaid it. Mary once mislaid hers, didn't you, Mary?"

"Yes, I was working in soapy water and it slipped off my finger. It can happen quite easily. I'll go and get it."

"Would you not like to sit down," said the minister. How odd it was that the girl should come back, he had never thought that she would. In a strange way he wished that she hadn't. And yet that was certainly not the Christian attitude to take. Even now, embarrassed and pale as she was, there emanated from her a strong sexual power which was quite unforced and almost primitive. Life would be difficult for her for a while, there was no question about that. But how had she been so stupid as not to foresee her own weakness and frailty? His wife came back with the ring which was in a little green box and which rested on cotton wool.

"We kept it safe," she said cheerfully. "It's perfectly all right. It looks quite expensive too."

"Yes, it was," said the girl taking the ring and slipping it on to her finger. "John paid a lot for it."

For a moment the minister saw in his wife's eye a glint which could only be described as envy, for the girl's ring was far more expensive than her own but it passed as quickly as it had come. The faithful suffer and the unfaithful profit, he thought.

"Everything is all right now?" he said carefully.

"Yes, everything is all right." He had an instinctive feeling that the girl would start coming to church. He didn't know how he knew this but he was quite convinced of it and the thought troubled him with great sadness.

The girl hesitated as if not quite sure how to go about leaving the room. What was he expected to say to her?

His wife suddenly remarked, "I'm going in your direction to visit Mrs Campbell. Can I give you a lift?"

"That's very kind of you," said the girl.

"Come on then. I'll get my coat," said Mary, and the two of them went out together leaving the minister alone.

He stood staring after them for a while, his mind turbulent and excited, and yet deflated. It was as if the weight of the village had settled on his shoulders again, as if he was overwhelmed by it. Why could she not have stayed where she was, have accepted what had happened to her, lived off the chances of the day? And then another voice said to him, "She left her children behind, not to mention her husband. You should be glad the repentant sinner has returned to the fold."

But he could not be glad, something in him felt melancholy and defeated: there was a smell of sickness and nausea in his mouth. When he heard the car he went to the bathroom and was sick. There was no end to the pain in the world, to the imperfection, to the ridiculousness, to the meaninglessness. How could he be a minister when he considered that the girl's return was a defeat for the human spirit? How could he possibly think in that way when she was so clearly a sinner, one who by her own selfishness had brought this sorrow on herself? And yet that part of him which thought of the human spirit conquering mountain after mountain from the time that man had first moved, hunchbacked and heavy jawed, about the plains and woods of the mornings, was offended. He drank some water and wiped his face and mouth with a towel. He went down on his knees among the alternate white and black squares of the bathroom and prayed. Please help me, O Lord, please help me. I've tried to be Thy servant but I am confused. Give me a sign, O Lord. Speak to me out of this terrible silence. This sterility. While he was praying he remembered Hutton who had asked the undertaker for the ring to be removed from his wife's finger. Had that been love or greed? How could one tell?

O Lord, he went on, I do not understand the human heart. I wish to be Thy servant but I feel nothing.

He rose from the floor, his knees aching and sore. All he could do was endure as those men had once endured the hailstones and the snow, plunging into the battle, knowing there was no final victory, till in the spring there came from the woods the pure clear lonely voice of the cuckoo, its double note.

What was there about Hutton's wife that he was forgetting? Had the finger been broken to get the ring off?

III

25

THE PLACE THEY had chosen for their picnic was a flat stretch of land near the water though not near enough to be dangerous to the children: and in the distance they could see the mountain ascending into a clear sky, for the weather remained miraculously clear and warm. The ground was dry enough for the adults to sit round the perimeter while the children ran their races. When the minister arrived (for his wife had been there before him) he looked at the scene in front of him. At one end of the field he could see Mary Macarthur beside Annie, while Murdo Macfarlane and David Collins were talking to each other. The Jap was there with his wife, child, and camera, while the German and his wife were sitting on the ground, the husband clad in shorts. Mrs Scott and her husband were standing at the table on which the sandwiches and lemonade were, as also were his own wife, Mrs Campbell, Patricia (Mrs Berry's daughter) and Elizabeth. Christine Murray and her husband were kneeling on the ground hand in hand at a little distance from the others. It was two o'clock in the afternoon and the sun was white in the sky.

From behind the table the minister spoke briefly.

"I'm glad," he said, "to see so many of you here. As you know, this is a Sunday School picnic but we have extended it so that as many as possible of the villagers will have the opportunity to be present. I haven't seen my wife for days now as she has been preparing sandwiches"—they laughed politely—"and I am glad to offer my thanks to all those who have prepared the food and drink. I think we can start now."

"What is he saying?" Mary Macarthur asked Annie.

"He is saying that the races can start now," said Annie. "He is praising his wife as usual. I see that Chrissie Murray is here. Do you notice her sitting over there beside her husband?" Annie had recently taken to wearing strings of brown beads, and bangles round her wrists, and was dressed in a brown frock.

"Yes, I see her," said Mary Macarthur, "maybe we should go and speak to her."

"Not just now," said Annie, "I am not sure that I wish to speak to her at this moment. Later perhaps I shall speak to her."

She watched the children lining up for the first race while the janitor tried to keep them in a reasonably straight row. These were the youngest children and among them was Mrs Berry's grandchild Peter, and Mrs Campbell's son, Malcolm. The Jap had raised his camera and was focussing it on them, as they giggled among themselves and looked down at each other's feet. Annie was sure that competition was not necessary in Eastern religions.

The janitor said, "Ready, steady, go," and they were all running in a disorderly manner towards the minister who was standing at the other end of the field, some with teeth gritted as if they were running in an important race such as they had seen on TV, and some with careless steps as if in a dream of their own. Two of them fell on the grass and rolled over and over shrieking with merriment, while the first to reach the finishing line was Peter.

"How is it that Peter always wins the race? He did the same last year," said Mrs Drummond to Mrs Berry.

"His grandfather was the same," said Mrs Berry abruptly. "He was good at running and throwing the caber. He was very strong." The children had now disentangled themselves from the confused mass they had formed at the finishing line and the minister was announcing the winner. Mrs Berry felt in her bones the pride she had felt once in her husband's running and feats of strength. Why, when his own brother had once challenged Angus to a fight the latter had beaten him with ease, though his brother, Iain, had been two stones heavier.

"I don't wish to see his wife gloating over you," she had hissed at him. "I can't stand her. She thinks the sun rises in her backside. Have you seen the new watch she's wearing? She's flashing it at me every time she can. You go in there and beat him." And the two of them had wrestled in the garden, she remembered, with the flowers all in bloom around them. At first it had seemed that his brother would beat him but then she had seen Angus's face reddening and the veins standing out on his forehead like thin ropes and he had made a tremendous heave and thrown his brother like a sack of potatoes across the lawn to land among the rhododendrons. She had turned and looked his wife straight in the eye and that had been the sweetest revenge of her life. And then there had been the other time when he had taken part in the races in Mull . . .

Peter came running towards her, the ten pence piece clutched in his sweaty hand. "You've done well," she said proudly. "You've kept up your grandfather's reputation," and he stood in front of her like a little sturdy boxer. Mrs Drummond and her husband had already left and were now standing beside Annie and Mary Mac-arthur. She knew perfectly well that the only reason that they had gone was because they were jealous of her grandson winning the race: they themselves were childless.

As she stood there with her hand resting on Peter's blond head she saw the Jap crossing the field towards her. He walked with short quick steps and his moon face beamed at her.

"Please," he said, pointing at the two of them and then at the camera. "Please."

She was reminded of the black man who had used to sell clothes out of a suitcase many years ago when she and Angus had been young. He had laid out on the floor socks, cardigans, handkerchiefs, pyjamas, nightgowns, and she had stared at them enviously and then said to Angus, "No, they're no good," though she had in fact liked them, but she couldn't afford them. The Jap was smiling uncertainly at her as if he were one of those people who expected to be rebuked when he asked for a favour, but then of course this was not his country, and how would she feel if she was in Japan?

She took Peter by the hand and she smiled at the Jap, at the same time telling Peter to stand still and look at the kind man who was taking his photograph. They said that those Japs were very clever and worked hard and copied our whisky and our tweed but after all it was a Sunday School picnic and God intended us to be kind to all his creatures even though some of them were yellow and some were black. She smiled, the camera clicked, the Jap bowed as if she were a queen, and then walked back with his quick steps to where his tiny wife was waiting with her unnaturally polite son.

By this time the second race had been run and Helen had come in second last and Hugh, the butcher's son, had won it and Alisdair was crying and stamping on the ground with his feet.

"I won it," he was shouting at the minister. "I won it." His mother ran out and hauled him back among the crowd lining the field, her face red with embarrassment but Alisdair was still stamping the ground crying.

"You bad boy," she was saying while the people turned away. "You bad boy."

"I'm not, I'm not," said Alisdair through his tears. "He's always winning, getting . . ."

And he couldn't continue with whatever he was going to say, for at that moment Elizabeth ran up with a bag of sweets from which she gave him one. Meanwhile Kenny Foolish was running by himself in a corner of the field, throwing his hands in the air, in a grotesque imitation of someone running a race on TV.

"He gets . . ." And Alisdair choked on the words while his mother slapped his bottom and made him cry louder. "When I get you home," she was saying, while Elizabeth offered him a striped sweet thinking how Alisdair's trousers had a patch on them and his mother had brought him up on her own after her husband had been struck by lightning while sitting on top of a telegraph pole, for he had been a Post Office engineer. But Alisdair was spitting the sweet out of his mouth and still shouting as if he was in some kind of fit. He danced on the ground with rage, his face swollen. "He'll be all right," said Mrs Mason to Elizabeth. "He'll be all right . . . It's just that . . ." And her voice trailed away. But the spectators had turned to the last of the three races in which the older children were taking part.

"There's another race to come," said Elizabeth to Alisdair. "You can dress up and then we can see if you will win. See, you can get into the wheelbarrow and John Murray will wheel you along and we'll see if you can win. Aren't you looking forward to that?" Alisdair suddenly stopped crying and smiled at her and Mrs Mason was jealous of this girl who had so easily quietened her son. But she didn't say anything as Elizabeth continued,

"And you'll get lemonade and a bun. You'll like that." And she walked across the grass to where the minister was standing at the table.

"We used to have races in the Army," said David Collins to Murdo. "One unit would be running against another unit. We called them units. That was in Aldershot." Already he was growing tired of the races and thinking of other things.

Murdo pretended not to hear him. He was tired of the Angel of Mons, the trenches, the guns, the Germans. He should never have come among these parents with their families, who was himself only a bachelor, and had never had a child in the cleansed and polished house in which he lived with his mother all those years.

"In Aldershot, that was," David Collins repeated, wiping the sweat from his face, "before we went off to France."

And it seemed to him that those days belonged to someone else, someone much younger than he was, someone totally different whose photograph, brown and blurred, he kept on the sideboard in his living room. Sometimes he would look at that photograph and think, "That's not me at all. It is a boy whom I used to know." He swiped angrily at a midge and thought, "The bloody Japs and Germans are everywhere. They are taking over the world." The Jap's camera had disturbed him. For a moment there when it had whirred it was as if he were hearing a hissing sound like a lit fuse running back to its source, the dangerous snake.

"Hullo, Alisdair," he said awkwardly. "Is it yourself? You should have won that race right enough." He put his hand in his pocket and took out a hard white sweet. "You take that," he said. "You eat that." Alisdair wonderingly took the sweet and then ran away on little fat legs. In a short while Murdo saw the two of them—Hugh and Alisdair—talking animatedly to each other. Nothing lasted long at that age, sunshine was followed by storm, storm by sunshine.

I'm not feeling too well, the minister thought, I should really sit down. I should be a different man for this job, I should be like the previous minister. No wonder the congregation preferred him to me. He was hail-fellow-well-met, a big red-faced man like a farmer who shouted at the congregation, "You are all rotten apples, you are bad potatoes." And then he would stalk about the fields, commenting on the state of the fruit and the vegetables, and they loved him. I on the other hand was never a sportsman, I never won a race in my life. I never took part in the cricket games in my school, the PT man was a brutal fellow who had played rugby for a first class team and he used to tell the boys the best methods of bringing someone down. "Don't be frightened," he would shout at them, "or I'll have your guts for garters." All those bony knees, dirty stockings, tiled washrooms. No, to be a minister one must live in the world, there's a way of talking that a congregation understands.

He passed his hand across his eyes, watching the crowd of people, seeing Chrissie and her husband sitting by themselves. There was a rightness about that too, the others would be leaving them together till she had adjusted to being home. They had their own tact which was instinctive and mannerly. In front of him he saw the Saxons with their wall of shields while the Vikings approached them in the white frosty morning. They were being cut to pieces but one of them was standing there and shouting, "The spirit will grow stronger", as the shields fell, as they yielded inch after inch. They are running towards me and I should receive them. Suffer the little children to come unto me . . .

Mary was standing beside him now and she was saying, "I think you should announce that the sports will stop for a while while we serve the lemonade and the sandwiches and the buns." He made the announcement and watched them forming themselves into a queue while some of the children were spinning round and round, chasing each other and falling on the grass. What energy they had at that age, what unclouded vision.

He removed the paper from a sandwich and began to eat it. As he was doing this his eye happened to catch that of a spectacled boy who was standing by himself at the edge of the field. He knew at once who it was, it was the Allison boy who was supposed to be the most brilliant scholar the school had ever had. His father and mother were rather odd people, incomers of course, who had a large untidy house a good bit out of the village, and who, according to local rumour, spent their time painting and sculpting and generally messing about with aesthetic materials. As well as this they ate only health food. Curiously enough they came to church every Sunday in an old battered car which was filled with bric à brac of various descriptions, and wearing clothes which reminded the congregation of those worn by hippies. The father who was English (as was the mother as well) was supposed to have been a scientist and to have invented a device from which others had got the benefit. Though they came to church they kept themselves to themselves and left immediately the service ended. They had however on one occasion organised a Bach evening which the locals had attended more out of curiosity than anything else but which afterwards they had criticised as not being, in their opinion, at the correct level for ordinary people.

Their son Henry was a spectacled boy with a bulging forehead who was a bit of a problem since he didn't mix with the other children, but who had the ability even at the age of twelve to discuss painting and music when the opportunity arose and whose knowledge of the geography of other countries which his parents had apparently visited was wide and detailed. In fact he frightened teachers for he was clearly so well in advance of the other pupils that it was rather embarrassing. However it appeared that his parents' views were such that they regarded a private education as out of the question, being firm believers in the comprehensive system and a 'normal' development for their child, ideas which they had pronounced with much eloquence at a Parents-Teachers' meeting.

It seemed to the minister as he watched the boy that Henry was studying the proceedings with a rather sceptical expression which he immediately hooded behind his round glasses when the minister looked at him. The latter was not surprised that the parents were not present nor that the boy had not taken part in any of the sports even though his age group had already run their race. He wondered vaguely what was going on in the boy's mind as he had often wondered in Sunday School when he had been explaining some passage in the Bible, for example the story of the Prodigal Son. The boy had been quite animated in maintaining that the father in the story had been rather unfair since he had so easily accepted his son back and even thrown a party for him when the older son had been so neglected. It occurred to the minister to wonder whether in fact Henry's father kept pigs. He certainly kept hens and sold their eggs. The boy had not been convinced by the minister's explanation that the story was not meant to be taken literally but was rather symbolic of man's relationship with God. The minister remembered the occasion very well as it was the only time that he had ever been forced into quite a hard argument, since the other children in the Sunday School were only there because their parents forced them to attend and were shy and reticent.

Henry, standing there so alone and so self assured, irritated him. It was as if his sceptical intelligence were a scandal to him. On an impulse he went over to talk to him.

"Good afternoon, Henry," he said pacifically.

"Good afternoon, sir."

"And what do you think of the proceedings, Henry?"

The boy turned on him an astonishingly intelligent smile and appeared to be about to say something illuminating but at the last minute as if out of good manners contented himself with saying,

"They seem to be going well, sir."

"We do this, Henry," said the minister, "in order to give everybody an outing at least once a year. I see that you didn't take part in the race."

"No, sir." The minister waited for the boy to volunteer some more information but Henry remained silent as if quite content with what he had already said. His self assurance and maturity were amazing. The minister felt in some way as if the picnic and himself and his church were all being judged in the light of an intelligence much superior to his own, and while standing there was amused by the spectacle of Kenny Foolish turning cartwheels on the other side of the field for the entertainment of the children. To the foolish all was revealed, though not necessarily to the bright.

Suddenly the boy said to him, "I was wondering, sir, what this had to do with the Bible."

The remark fell so easily and almost casually from his lips that the minister was at first unsure whether he had heard right and he stood still for a moment looking around him. Many of the people were now sitting on the grass, eating their sandwiches and drinking their lemonade, while in the distance he could see the mountain and to its left the sun, round and golden in the sky. A baby was crying in its mother's arms, David Collins was talking to Annie, his slightly unshaven face alight with interest in what she was saying. To his right he could see a boy and a girl walking into the wood which was on the opposite bank, the boy's arm around the girl's waist. He imagined them speaking lovingly to each other or remaining silent while they walked, while the leaves of the trees stirred in the slight breeze. He imagined them lying down in a glade somewhere in the half light and shadow of the wood, the boy perhaps spreading a jacket beneath the girl while they kissed each other and the only noises to be heard were those of the twittering of the birds and the murmur of the river.

It was as if a door had been slightly opened but not wide enough, for almost as soon as it happened the vision was gone, and he felt frustrated and bad-tempered again. For a moment there he could have walked casually through the door into a country which would have revealed to him once and for all the secret of life and of existence, but it had closed as suddenly as it had opened and all he could see was his wife and Elizabeth and Mrs Scott and Mrs Campbell at the table to which various people came for more sandwiches and lemonade, and their bodies were opaque and obdurate again. He noticed that John Murray and Chrissie were still sitting by themselves on the rim of the proceedings. Maybe he should go over and talk to them but he didn't feel ready as yet.

He turned towards the boy as if to answer his statement but found that the words would not form in his mouth. He might have said glibly that the connection between sports and the Bible was that the former were intended to bring the villagers together in a community which would attain a closer unity by them, but he felt that this was not a justification or indeed an explanation. I am like Wordsworth, he considered, I am ending my life in the light of common day. Once there was a radiance to which the rainbow and the rose and the worn hands contributed, now there is only the ordinary daylight on which the shadows of people fall without the poetry of ideas. And yet he felt himself on the edge of a revelation which however was not quite descending on him, as were not the twenty-four elders of whom Annie spoke. Why, even David Collins had often spoken of the angel of Mons which he had seen, according to himself, so many years ago from the shelter of the infested trenches. But all he could see as he looked around him were people eating sandwiches and drinking lemonade. There was Mrs Berry sitting beside her daughter Patricia, who had left the table for a moment while beside them sitting on the ground were Peter and Helen. There was the German and his wife, both munching contentedly, while the Jap and his wife and son were also eating as if that was the correct thing to do in a strange country. There was Kenny Foolish, upside down like a fool in a Tarot pack, doing his eternal handstands and surrounded by a ring of laughing children.

When he turned back to Henry he knew that he didn't have an answer to give him, not now at any rate, and for a moment he hated the closed smart sceptical intelligence, observing and watching, as if it were his own. The fact that the boy didn't take part in sports was another sign of his separation from the ordinary world, however powerful his mind was, and he suddenly felt like cursing his parents who had all the right ideas but not the right feelings. What was the use of being anti-nuclear, pro-sufficiency-farming if they did not feel the necessary pain and sorrow and joy which would only come from an immersion in the poor dumb meagre and sometimes marvellous world?

His gaze wandered from the boy to the buzzard perched on a fence near him and he saw as if with horror the eternally questing head, the absolute patience. They had all said that David Collins had been devastated by the death of his cat which had evaded for so many years the dangers of the traffic but which had at last by a curious random justice been killed by a motorist who hadn't even stopped. The cat had apparently died in David's lap, one eye hanging down, the other open and seemingly aware of where it was, or at least that was what David had said.

"It was as if he knew me. It was as if he was grateful that I was there." When the minister wakened as it were from his speculations he found that the boy had gone as if impatient that the answer he had been looking for had not been delivered to him. But the people were still eating and drinking on the large plain which adjoined the water. They had completely forgotten him. Even his wife was talking to Mrs Campbell, possibly asking her about her foreign lodgers, while Mrs Scott was debating something with Elizabeth. He had never felt less like the shepherd of a flock.

"In the East," Annie was saying to David, "they don't have strong feelings. They let the will waste away. I don't much care for this lemonade as it acidifies the stomach. I know that you don't like foreigners but you should forgive and forget. It is possible that you were a foreigner yourself in a previous existence. What it is necessary to see is that the Buddha sat under a tree, a tree just like that one," and she pointed while her bangles dangled at her wrist, "and he told us that there must be no evil in our hearts. I wonder what kind of pâté they have on these sandwiches. It has a fishy taste. You see, as a former member of His Majesty's Forces you still have evil in your heart. Countries cause wars, not persons. Have you thought about that? Your cat which I hear died recently might go into the body of a man. It would not surprise me if he became like Mrs Campbell. The Egyptians worshipped the cat as I have read in the Encyclopædias. You cannot go through life with hatred in your heart though I can understand it, all those boys dead in Flanders. I think we should go over and talk to those Germans, if they have any English, and I must say that I don't approve of men wearing shorts. They are as bad as the kilt. This ridiculous idea of trying to make oneself look young when one is old, I find it disgusting. Let us go over and talk to them: they appear lonely. And in any case that man was not born when you were in the trenches among the lice and the flies."

Masterfully she pulled David after her, her beads bouncing on her flat chest and her nose headed steadily towards the Germans.

It was, thought David, as if it was his mother's hand he felt in his own or perhaps the hand of Mary Macarthur long ago behind the school privy on a summer's day. The face of his friend Alasdair rose in front of him. He himself was running through the French wood, his rifle in his hand. Alasdair was lying there on the ground not yet dead but badly wounded. He should stop and save him but there was no hope, there was surely no hope. He ordered his feet to stop but they couldn't, they seemed to have a life of their own which didn't respond to his control. They were flying on regardless, away from the sun. He saw his boots among the leaves and now and again flashes of sheep on grazing land. Alasdair was hiding among the leaves and there were nest eggs everywhere, eggs the size of cannon balls, in the blue day. Let him find a nest and hide in it, a secret nest away from the guns, with brown speckled eggs in it.

He and Annie were now standing in front of the Germans who had risen to their feet immediately. The woman in a long decorated skirt smiled expectantly, the man was dabbing crumbs from his shorts. They were trying to frame words from their small treasury of English. Annie was going on and on. "Do you have Sunday School outings in Germany?" she was saying. "Of course they're quite useless. Of course Martin Luther is to blame for much that is wrong with the church nowadays. He should have listened more to the saints. It is only when we are thirsty and starved that we have revelations." The German nodded vigorously and his wife smiled uncertainly, and David thought, "I never saw a German with

lemonade stains on his shorts before. This man looks very clumsy."
He looked down at the lemonade bottle which was standing upright
on the ground. The bubbles rose and fell ceaselessly like an escalator.

"And another thing," Annie was saying, "the Buddha was
against all forms of violence. And as for that Hitler I never cared for
his moustache. Was it stuck on, do you think? It seemed to me that he
was like an actor, that someone had stuck the moustache on his
face . . ."

26

"I THINK IT is going very well," said Mary Murchison to Mrs Scott, as she handed a sandwich to a small boy who had come up to the table. Mrs Scott said that it was. And indeed it was going surprisingly well. The field was filled with people of all shapes and sizes, and colours of clothes. It was rather like a painting that she had once seen in the Art Gallery in Surrey though she couldn't now remember the painter's name. It had been painted on perhaps such a summer's day, not, she thought, in Britain but in Europe, perhaps France. And there was Gerald standing with Murdo Macfarlane; she wondered what they were talking about. "And I've an idea for an ending to the day," said the minister's wife. "It is always a good thing to end the day on a high note," and smiled at her secret pun. It occurred to Mrs Scott that there might be a fruitful argument about the money that would be left over from the Sale of Work when the lemonade and the sandwiches had been paid for. She thought that perhaps it might be used for the petrol expenses of those who were doing the Meals on Wheels. She turned to say something to Mary Murchison but the latter had walked away and was talking to Elizabeth.

She stood there uncertainly, isolated at the table, apart from the minister who seemed to be lost in a dream after he had been talking to that strange boy Henry Allison. If she were in Surrey, now, what would she be doing? She thought that perhaps she would be drinking coffee with Isa Weaver in the tea shop over which that grey-haired woman presided. She tried to remember her name but couldn't and she was bothered by that. Her mind circled the alphabet alighting on a letter here and there but in spite of all her efforts she couldn't trap the name. Good Lord, she thought, what is happening to me. Not so long ago she would have been able to recall the name without difficulty and also the exact appearance of that thatched cottage that stood at the corner of the street with its small leaded panes. But she couldn't even remember what colours the panes were. Now, wasn't that odd? It must be significant in some way. She shivered slightly as if, in Mrs Berry's words, someone was walking on her grave. The proceedings had come to a stop for a moment and in that hiatus she stood miserably in the middle of nowhere half way between Surrey and the village, as if she were at a station from which the train had already departed. And then she caught sight of John Murray and Chrissie still sitting by themselves in a corner of the field, their two children among the others who were playing happily having forgotten the adults. On an impulse she went over to them, a sandwich and lemonade in her hand. Crossing the field she was aware of no eyes looking at her and was happy in her privacy. It was as if they had all accepted that she should be in the position she was in, authoritative and efficient. Well, wasn't she those things? Hadn't she been efficient all her days? All that she wanted in return was some recognition of her efforts. The shadows slanted away from her as she walked across the field, a harvest of shadows.

She knelt down in front of John Murray and his wife and said, "Would you like some lemonade and a sandwich?" Murray looked at her gratefully and Chrissie immediately took the sandwich.

"Thank you very much," they both said.

"It's a fine day," she said. "Isn't it fortunate that it has turned out nice? I had misgivings about the whole thing but I'm glad to confess that I was wrong."

Now that she was beside them she didn't know what to say and kept her talk to the weather which at least wouldn't probe at raw wounds. She noticed that Chrissie was wearing a longer skirt than usual and that her hair was coiled at the back of her head in a bun. The ring was back on her hand. So she too was adapting to her new circumstances. The tribe must be placated, the mysterious price must be paid. The tribe was like a living organism which swallowed its components and waxed and waned accordingly. She saw it as a spongey jellyfish placidly drifting in briny water.

"I hear you're in the wheelbarrow race," she said to John.

"Yes, I got myself landed for that," he replied. She wondered what would happen to Chrissie while he was taking part in the sports and decided that she would stay with her.

The grass below her was slightly damp. Not far from her she saw the Jap smiling into the sun serene as a graven image. Her mind cast about for a topic that would be neutral enough for the inflammation not to become swollen again. And yet there was a compulsion, sadistic in its intensity, to be probing at the wound.

"It is good for the children to have such a day," she said at last to Chrissie who replied, "Yes, it brings them together doesn't it?" Yet even that statement, innocent as it appeared, hadn't been a neutral one for it recalled that Chrissie had in fact been willing to abandon her children when she had made her frantic flight.

On the other hand how could one remain silent, thought Mrs Scott. One could only do that when the atmosphere around one was settled and calm. She noticed that Chrissie was wearing flat shoes and not the red flamboyant boots in which she had left the village. Well, what had it been like? She herself had often speculated about such a parting, even from her own husband, steady and unwavering as he was. There was a part of her which remained discontented with the kitchen and the cooker, the white shrine at which so many were forced to serve. There was a part of her which was fluttering and wild and dumb. Not that she had ever made the leap though she had thought about it: not that her husband had ever dreamed that she would make it.

The minister was now announcing the wheelbarrow race in which the children would be wheeled along by the stronger adults. John stood up, excused himself, and walked across the field to where the wheelbarrows were waiting. In one of them Kenny Foolish was hanging upside down as if on a playful cross which he had devised for himself. The wheelbarrows were brought to the starting point with lazy movements as if they were stirring in a gluey substance composed of time become tactile.

Mrs Scott suddenly turned to Chrissie and asked, "What was it like, then?" It was as if she were saying, "We are two outsiders, you might as well tell me and I won't tell anyone. We both made the leap, I to this village which I saw at its best during the summer holidays, you to that man whose better side you saw."

"I made a mistake," said Chrissie, "I made a bad mistake." It was the first time that she had spoken of what had happened since she came home. Everyone was trying to avoid speaking of the business and now this Englishwoman with the blunt nature was asking her. Her voice seemed to herself dead and far away.

"It was all right at the beginning. It's a great feeling to throw everything away. I did it on impulse. One day I was washing dishes

126

at the sink and I could see the mountain in front of me and the train going up and down and then I . . . just went. It was like a brainstorm. I'm glad I came back."

"Are you? Are you?" said Mrs Scott fiercely. "Are you sure?"

"Yes, I'm sure," Chrissie replied, calmly. "I'm perfectly sure."

And she was sure. She felt at home in a way that she had never felt at home in Glasgow. She couldn't put into words what exactly she felt, it was a peace that almost justified her momentary exile.

She looked across to the water which shone in the sun and then to her right where she could see Mrs Berry's calf grazing in the field, tethered there by its rope. In a way it was all like that, necessary and to be chafed against. The only thing that bothered her was that she had to make her hair into a bun, she who had before her marriage worked as a hairdresser and who hated such conformity. And yet she wasn't to be pitied. She was in fact very lucky. What if after all John hadn't wanted her back? But he had done so in spite of everything, in spite of the knowledge of that other bed in which she had so feverishly rested, in spite of the betrayal. That must be what people called love.

She watched him as he placed little Alisdair in the wheelbarrow, lifting him lightly and carefully. How had she not recognised that patient fidelity? The shadow fell over her again. What if he had not wanted her back? What if in the future he wanted someone else? What would her bargaining power be then?

"Don't you worry," said Mrs Scott patting her knee. "Don't worry. Time will heal. You will have to join one of our committees. It will keep you from being bored. Once you've heard Mrs Campbell going on for an hour you'll feel that you're at home again." And she laughed happily as if she and Mrs Campbell belonged inalienably to the same village, equal and essential to each other.

Chrissie smiled back at her. What a pretty child she was, though later she would almost certainly run to fat.

"You and John come and see us one night. We'll have plenty to talk about."

The diamond panes on that thatched cottage, had they been red or green? And had the woman's name been Sarah or . . . She could swear that it began with an S. Now she could see the bus shelter and hear the birds singing in the gardens. She was standing at the station and the train was rocketing past at what must have been eighty miles an hour. She withdrew from the edge of the platform. There was an Indian standing beside her, a furled umbrella in one hand and a copy of *The Times* in the other. No, she couldn't go back there, it was finished with, it was a world that was forever gone. She must put all that away from her, and accept the place where she was as being the one where she would stay and be eventually buried. There was no way round it, the railway lines had pointed irretrievably to where she was.

The Jap was standing up with his camera pointed at the wheelbarrows and Mrs Berry was standing beside her daughter Patricia, her green cap on her head. And there was Annie talking to those Germans in her circles of brown beads, her hawklike face vital and interested as if she belonged to a world that was definite and meaningful. The sun laid a track across the field and the wheelbarrows were about to go.

"Come on, come on!" the minister heard himself shouting to John Murray who was wheeling Alisdair along in the barrow. All around him there was shouting and cheering as the competitors raced across the field bouncing in and out of the slight hollows of deeper damper green in the ground. At the far end of the line which was advancing raggedly yet energetically he could see Peter, Mrs Berry's grandson, in a barrow which was being wheeled along by the janitor, Duncan Bell, known affectionately as the Furnace. He hadn't realised that there were so many wheelbarrows in the village, all painted in different colours, all seemingly in good condition. It recalled the chariots of the—was it the Hittites?—who had in the past attacked the Egyptians and beaten them down from their arrogant power. The race seemed to him to be symbolic of an army as it headed into the sun which was shining directly ahead. It was odd how involved for a moment he felt in the fortunes of these wheelbarrow drivers, even though they were slightly comic, the wheelbarrows like parodies of war machines composed of brittle wood, while the crowd laughed and cheered, some of them with sandwiches still in their hands. And there it was. The momentary justice of life had decreed that John Murray and Alisdair should win. (Had the janitor in fact slowed down slightly at the decisive moment?) But Alisdair was now out of the wheelbarrow and dancing up and down in triumph, his previously petulant face transformed from anger into joy. Suffer the little children to come unto me, the Lord had said, in their changeable hearts, in their almost uncorrupted shine of the future. In just such a place as this, among such a crowd, He had preached, while later there had been gathered the remains of the fishes and the loaves, the eternally renewed bread of the imagination. How lucky it was that both John Murray and Alisdair had at last won, and how the crowd liked it. His wife was now bending down and handing Alisdair his ten pence and Alisdair was running away to his friends, his face alight with happiness.

He walked over towards Mary Macarthur who was sitting by her self on a chair that someone had thoughtfully supplied. He thought that it was Mrs Campbell who had thought of bringing chairs along for the older people and made a mental note to thank her.

"And how are you today?" he asked, leaning down, for Mary was slightly deaf.

"Oh, I'm fine, minister," she replied, her face creased yet happy and serene. How old would she be now? Climbing for eighty certainly.

"Good, good," he heard himself saying. "And how are you enjoying your little outing?"

"It's fine, minister. My daughter couldn't come. I wish she had been able to come." Of course she couldn't come, she was married to a Catholic. "I miss her," she added petulantly. "But then she belongs to the Other Side."

"Yes," he said, "I quite understand."

The old woman tapped the arms of her chair spiritedly and said furiously, "He wouldn't let her come, you know, even though her place is here."

"But of course," said the minister placatingly, "her children don't come to the Sunday School."

"I know that but they should, shouldn't they? Didn't I go myself to the Sunday School when Mr Marshall was the minister here? And didn't she herself go to the Sunday School? In those days you had to do what your parents told you."

She was staring at him with an odd almost disquieting gaze, and he felt that she knew things about him that he didn't know himself. She had a reputation for telling fortunes in the village, and many superstitious women had gone to visit her to have their fortunes read from her study of tea leaves; she had once cured little Alisdair of what she called the King's Evil, a spot on his lip. The minister himself didn't believe in such nonsense though curiously enough his wife had had her fortune read on one of her visits to the old woman.

She had looked at her cup and tilted it this way and that and said that there was a bit of jealousy going on around her, and that she could see a voyage. She was perfectly convinced of her own powers. The same unwinking stare—common to both the old and children—was fixed on him.

"You are not well," she told him at last as if delivering a weighty judgment. "You should look after yourself." Her voice came to him as the Oracle at Delphi must have come to the Greeks and behind her he could see, stretched into a far past, a history of witchcraft and magic from which the church had managed to extricate itself.

"Oh, I'm all right," he said lightly.

"Of course you have much to do," she said. "The Catholics are taking over the world. Did you see the pictures of the Pope on TV? You have to stop them," she said leaning towards him confidentially. "Mr Marshall never gave them an inch, not that much," and she measured a tiny length on her finger. "He preached against them regularly. He called them the Powers of Darkness. Now my son-in-law belongs to them. He worships that holy water and he makes my daughter go to Mass. You watch them, that Pope is a cunning devil. In his white robes."

"I look after myself," he said in the same light tone.

"You don't understand," she insisted. "You don't understand, I wouldn't be surprised if that Mrs Scott wasn't one of them. We don't watch them enough." And then she added, "You should take honey. Honey is good for you. It has the sun in it."

At that moment he had the strangest feeling as if he had actually been touched by an omen from the darkness and roots of long ago, an ancient force which dwelt in this woman who refused to eat fish because the Catholics were supposed to eat it. It was as if the field itself darkened and on one side of it there were the phantom warriors for good, arrayed in their white robes, while ranged against them on the other side were the warriors of evil emerging out of the shadows that played around them. The field became a treasury of herbs among which old women bent down to gather the most secret in order to help their own army. He shivered in the sun and said,

"Well, I'm glad that John Murray and little Alisdair won."

"Yes, he's a good joiner. It's a pity about that wife of his in her Papish boots. But he's a good man and a good worker. And Alisdair's mother hasn't had much since her husband was killed." How old the woman was. Perhaps she was more than eighty. Her face was beginning to curdle like old milk.

Was it true that even in this village in the past people had stuck pins into effigies of those whom they hated, that this woman herself could still cure the King's Evil as kings had done in the past?

"I'm sorry," he said, "I'll have to go. I'd better announce the next event," which was in fact a three-legged race.

"You take honey," she said, smiling at him. "You take honey. It's the best thing you can take."

"I'll do that," he replied. "I'll make sure my wife buys honey next time she goes shopping."

And yet the meeting with the old woman had disturbed him. It was as if through her he sensed an ancient force, which was indifferent both to evil and to good, which was close to the sources of nature itself in all its manifestations, whose badge was perhaps the oak tree and whose instruments were herbs and nostrums of all kinds. He prayed rapidly as if to make the darkness pass from him and thought wryly that if he had been a Catholic he might have counted his beads.

"I am certain," said Mrs Campbell to him, "that John Murray and Alisdair were allowed to win that race. I don't think that's fair."

"Oh, I never noticed that," he said diplomatically.

"I could see Duncan Bell," she said. "He pulled back at the last minute. That was because Alisdair lost his first race and made a fuss about it. My daughter was in the race, you know. And my husband couldn't get past Duncan Bell when he pulled back. I am quite sure that is what happened."

"If you are convinced that is what happened perhaps you should have a word with Duncan himself."

"Duncan? Of course he would deny it. He would deny everything. He has no sense of truth whatsoever."

It occurred to the minister that the reason she didn't like Duncan

Bell was that they both competed for Bed and Breakfast visitors. There was also the fact that Mrs Campbell had been a teacher before her marriage and considered Duncan Bell to be many classes below her.

"That man thinks he runs the school," she would say. "He has more power than the headmistress herself." And indeed one would think that too from talking to Duncan who would say, "My school has the worst ceilings in the county. When I 'phoned him up the Director of Education said that he couldn't do anything about them. I told him that I considered my school to be as important as any in the county. I told him that over the 'phone."

"I should just like to know," said Mrs Campbell. "If we are going to have competitions let us have fair competitions. It's the principle of the thing."

The minister briefly made the announcement about the three-legged race and standing with his back to the table stood and watched. He felt very tired as if his whole body had turned to water, and yet there was an hour or so yet to go. He looked forward to a night at the fire reading a book. The last time he had been to the library he had a strange feeling as if he were walking over skulls and the bones of millions of people, as if as a minister he should not be studying books but listening to endless stories of tragedy and sickness.

He looked over towards Elizabeth. Now there was a girl of plain shining goodness. What money she made at her job she spent the greater part of on Oxfam, and yet he himself had recently read that hardly any of that money was getting through to the victims. They said that parcels meant for the poor and dispossessed were being stolen by those who were organising the supplies. Bespectacled, cheerful, pale, Elizabeth was always helping people in the village, but was considered by Mary Macarthur to be in the pay of the Catholics because she had brought her fish on a Friday.

He was suddenly filled with anger. Was there no end to the petty strategies of the mind, was there no end to its vanity and egotism and its thorny sensitivity? Was there no end to the eternal voice that cried, "I am, I am, look at me. I will not be put upon."

He felt as if he wished to leave the assembled crowd and go away somewhere, and then it came to him, "This must have been how

Christ Himself felt when He went into the desert to pray. Underneath the stars. He must have grown exhausted by unteachable human nature with its coil on coil of self deceit, He must have tried to put the voices away from Him and lain on the ground at night staring up at the lucid cities of the stars, so aloof and so apparently harmonious." But then he was a minister, he wasn't Christ, he was only a poor follower, he needed help.

How could God have made such people the apex of his creation, how could He have generated out of the immense ocean of His illimitable spirit people whose worry was that a wheelbarrow race had been fixed? And he suddenly smiled to himself as he thought that perhaps he was being too serious. Perhaps he should look more towards a solution of comic glory, as if the whole universe were a healthy joke the answer to whose complexities would finally emerge like the punch line in a funny story.

27

MARY MURCHISON WAS not an imaginative person. It did not occur to her when she watched the three-legged race that there was anything at all symbolic in it, two people limping along chained to each other heading for the same goal. As she watched her husband talking now to one person now to another she was concerned first of all by his appearance (had he for instance polished his shoes or had he forgotten to put his shirt inside his trousers?), but these days she was also worried about more than that. For of course she knew what the doctor had told him, she was not foolish enough not to know that there was something wrong. Nor did she speculate, as she might have done if she had been more intellectual, that there might be a profound connection between his loss of faith and his cancer, one causing the other, though the enigma was like that of the chicken and the egg. For reasons of his own he did not wish to tell her, he was protecting her in his own fashion and she respected him for what he was doing.

There was a part of his personality which was forever shut to her, his omnivorous love of books and ideas and language. She was not herself a bookish person for quite simply she did not have the time to read. Nor did she consider books all that important. She thought of them rather as shadows of the real world in which one had to wash, cook, make one's way with people. It never occurred to her that he should not have become a minister, for she felt that his only handicap was his shyness. Before she married him she had been a nurse of a younger generation than Mrs Berry's and she was not likely not to know that he was ill. She had been a nurse in a geriatric hospital as well and though the patients there had delusions of permanent love and power, she would not have thought like Mrs Berry that to live in a world of dreams was a good thing for them, for she had come from a long line of ancestors who had fought in the real world for religious principle, her father having been a minister as well. She knew however that the ministry had changed from those days, that no one threatened passive congregations with the fires and tortures of hell as had happened in the past.

Her own faith was of a different order. She simply rested quite easily in the meaningfulness and sense of the world. God was like a housekeeper for Whom everything was in its place in an eternal busy kitchen. He could put His hand on anything when He wanted to.

There was no one in the village whom she disliked, for they were what they were and that was what could be said about them. The sanity of the world was its most important characteristic. It was true that recently she had been under considerable strain since her husband, though he was unaware of it, had begun to talk in his sleep, something which he had never done in the past. Suddenly he would cry out as if he were being attacked or as if he were lost on a road whose end he could not foresee. One night he had got up and walked about the chilly manse in his sleep muttering to himself in a language that she couldn't understand, as if it were Hebrew or Greek or some idiom that only the unconscious could speak.

It had never occurred to her to love anyone else but him: her faithfulness was absolute. There were times she regretted not seeing more of her children but she must place her husband before them, especially now when the wheels of his being were running low and he was living on the energy of the past. As she watched the three-legged race the sort of thing she thought about was, 'That handkerchief is not tied tightly enough: how could one be so clumsy and inefficient?' She did not expect great miracles in her life nor did she think that when the day was over she would gather in more food than she had put out. Her image of Christ was of an infinitely good but sane and practical person who dealt with the people with compassion and good sense and was aware of their limitations. She did not see him surrounded by a halo of transcendent beauty—the beauty that was never yet on sea or land—but rather walking about Galilee with an energetic purposefulness that she could easily understand. Nor at the same time did she find it difficult to understand that He had been crucified. People were malicious on one level but on another level they could show the most amazing generosity as had happened for instance when Alisdair's father had been killed. It was true that later they might cavil about this or that but in their very depths they wanted to be good. It was an instinct.

One of the people she most admired was Elizabeth who without fuss or ego did as much as she could for the village. She gave most of her salary to Oxfam and visited the old, the sick, and frail. It never occurred to Mary that she herself was doing much the same as Elizabeth for she considered her work a duty. Loving came more easily to her than to her husband. Loving for him was a perpetual struggle, an inarticulate desire. It was as if he considered it a weakness which had to be expiated and paid for. He could hardly bring himself to say, "My dear", or "Darling", or even to touch her much in the course of the day and yet his faithfulness like hers was absolute. People recognised this remoteness in him but at the same time they respected him for they knew that he was always trying to do the right thing. There were in the world the divinely gifted ones on whom grace rested continually like a light from heaven and who moved like perfect athletes, and there were the other ones, whose every gift had to be fought for at the greatest expense of the spirit. Why must everything be so hard for him, why was there never an unexpected letter from the fields of harmony?

In comparison with her husband even David Collins and Murdo Macfarlane led easy lives, for they, like her, rested in the simplicities of the day. Even as she watched she saw Murdo, one-eyed and garrulous, talking earnestly to Mrs Campbell. His sense of duty had also been overwhelming but he was now proud of those demanding journeys. Her husband would never rest in pride. She would often pray on his behalf, "Let him be at peace even for a short time", but no answer had come to her one way or another. As she was thinking all this Mrs Johnstone's little daughter came over to her and pointed to her grazed knee. Mary bent down and touched it with her fingers very gently. "It will be all right. That bad knee. It will be all right." To deceive children was necessary, for to them the sharp stone and the thorn were evil and treacherous. It was so easy to cure them of their pain unless that pain was serious. She remembered again the apoplectic surgeon under whom she had trained, who had breezed his short-tempered way through the wards and whom the patients had instinctively loved, because he saw them and knew who they were. Clouds of minions followed him, adoring and disciplined, for he knew them too by name. His little shrewd eyes converted his work into a dramatic act which embraced all of them, though often he would swear at them and curse them. As she stroked the child's knee those days came back to her on a flood of fresh feeling.

The windows were wide open, the nurses in their blue úniforms walked among the beds, with their red coverlets. Thermometers were studied like tiny silver fish held up to the light, old becalmed men sat watching TV while flowers flourished triumphantly in bowls and vases. There were sounds of taxi doors slamming at night, laughter and song.

The race had ended and there was only one more left, till the finale she had chosen. But the lemonade bottles must be collected—they might get money on the empties. The janitor would have to take away the remains of the sandwiches. She was glad to see there were no fragments on the ground.

Kenny Foolish was standing beside her with his shining eyes. "How are you, Kenny," she said. He smiled back at her. He put out his hand and she gave him a sandwich, and his eyes lighted up.

"You like the sandwiches?" she asked. He nodded gratefully while at the same time he chewed the bread so loosely that she could see it soggy and half masticated in his loose mouth.

"Good," she said briskly as if she were a nurse in a hospital. "Good." And now here was Mrs Campbell. She would have some other complaint probably about the three-legged race. Mary lifted her eyes and saw, past the approaching Mrs Campbell, the mountain which rose into the sky at the back of the village.

I raise my eyes to the hills, she thought. From them comes my strength. Part of the sky was reddening now. In David Collins' field she saw the sheep grazing. To him at that moment Annie was talking intently and now and again raising her stick as if to indicate a sight that was of interest to them both.

Her husband was handing out ten pence each to the winners of the three-legged race whom she recognised as Tommy Matheson and Ewen Harrison. Past them and past the approaching Mrs Campbell she could see that clever bespectacled English boy, Henry, who was taking it all in, that scene which lay before him, and speculating on it. She wondered if in the future when she and her husband and most of the participants were dead, he would describe it to someone perhaps at the other end of the world.

In a corner of a field she heard a radio being played and decided that it must stop. For one thing it wasn't good for Chrissie, she might construe it as a subtle insult. In the future she would be known as Chrissie the Radio: these words would be her epitaph as fixed as if they had been written on marble: as if they had been carved on her tombstone.

SITTING BESIDE HUGH on the ground Alisdair said, "My mother says David Collins' cat is going to heaven. Do you think you'll go to heaven?"

"I'm going to heaven," said Hugh confidently. "But my father is going to the devil. My mum said so."

"Is that where you have to work?" said Alisdair seriously.

"I think so," said Hugh equally gravely. "You have to have a shovel . . . I'd rather go to heaven."

Alisdair put his hands together and prayed, "Please God, don't let me go to hell for I don't like working with a shovel. Do you think that's all right?"

"I think so," said Hugh swiping at a big white butterfly that swam past. "I think that's all right." He thought his own grandfather would be going to heaven soon for he had a wrinkled face and would find the cat in heaven and look after it.

AT FOUR O'CLOCK when the last event of the sports had taken place Mary Murchison stepped forward and said, "And now we have a little surprise for you. Elizabeth here will play on her guitar. She will of course play and sing religious songs. And now without any more ado, Elizabeth." The spectacled girl bent down and retrieved her guitar which was in its case on the table and strung it round her neck.

"She doesn't at all look like a guitarist," thought the minister. "She looks pale and rather nervous."

The boys and girls sitting on the grass or standing at the edge of the field clapped and she began to play. At first she played *Amazing Grace* and *When the Saints Go Marching In*, and the minister was surprised at the fire and enthusiasm with which she sang. Her pallor looked passionate and dedicated as if she had emerged in a dazzled manner into the power of her own talent. Behind her he could see the sun which was now lower in the sky and casting shadows across the field while in the far distance he could see the train winding its way like an undulating snake among the hills. It was with unexpected force that the vision came to him. In the background while she was playing he was aware of a child persistently crying. On the margin of his mind he was even wondering what Annie would think of the guitar-playing and more especially what Murdo's reaction would be. And then quite suddenly the vision came. Elizabeth was playing *Go Tell it On the Mountain*, the young people on the grass were swaying from side to side, the mountain ahead of him was tipped with flame and its veined dry watercourses were startlingly visible in the light as if they had leapt forward and become three-dimensional

> Go tell it on the mountain,
> over the hills and everywhere,
> Go tell it on the mountain
> that Jesus Christ is born . . .

At that exact moment it was as if he heard very distinctly a bell ringing in his mind like a telephone in an empty house. The sound of the bell became faint, and he began to fill slowly as if with water, very gravely, very seriously. The baby's cry had something to do with it. It was the guarantee of humanity itself. It wasn't that he saw angels in the sky, not David Collins' angel at Mons, not Annie's blazing twenty-four elders, not any winged clear-eyed angels at all. No, it was something very different from that. As his eyes, free and hawklike, scanned the people in the field it was as if he was overwhelmed by the pathos of their existence. He saw them each as separately and clearly as the shadows that were cast like solid black metal on the ground and he was aware that each of them was alone, and yet at that moment they were joined to each other by the power and joy of the music.

"Go tell it on the mountain," sang Elizabeth, bespectacled and pale. She too was a part of the proud humble company, which needed so much the happiness that the music created. "They are all like me, each one of them is like me," he thought with a sudden rapture, "I am not in any way apart from them, different from them. Whatever they suffer I suffer. We are together on this supremely imperfect and perfect earth. We are not looking for miracles, for the miracles do not happen. We are enduring but more than enduring. At moments we are touched by the crown of grace. Envious, jealous, embittered as some of us are the message is for us. The kingdom of heaven is at hand, it is here, it is all around us." And he had a vision of the people of the world, the fireman, the doctor, the lifeboatman, the minister. He saw tenement doors being broken down by axes, and the half dead receiving tea from extended hands. He saw at night the lifeboat heading out to sea in response to the call of those who were in danger of drowning. He saw the fire engine racing towards a fire, itself red as it, he saw stewardesses on 'planes walking confidently among the passengers. He saw the network which joined all those people, one to another, and he saw the village itself as a subtle structure like a spider's web on a summer's day, the spider existing on the justice of heaven.

All this he saw in a grave radiance illuminated by the sun, by the cry of the child. "We are united indissolubly," he thought, "as if we are part of a divine marriage, as if in a church we had taken each other by the hand and placed the ring on the finger, the ancient scarred ring." He was astonished by the water and light that poured through

him as if he were pregnant with faith. Christ walked among the
hedges, among the flowers of Galilee, beside a sea that was an
illimitable expanse, meagre and haggard and yet joyful. That wood
on which he had died was formed by some carpenter as ordinary as
John Murray, proud of his handiwork. There was an ironical
perfection about the world, it was overwhelmingly composed of
complexity and simplicity.

"Go tell it on the mountain," Elizabeth sang and he watched all
the people around.

"My love, my love," he thought as he gazed at his wife in that
vision of opening doors, "how much you have done for me. This love
between us is part of the love that created the sun and the other stars."

And he did not feel frightened at all when he saw Morag Bheag
approaching with a piece of yellow paper in her hand, though he
knew with amazing clarity what it was. It was curious how transparent his mind was; without being told he knew what the telegram
signified and the telegram itself became part of the whole network
that he was so sublimely aware of. It must be about her son, from
Ireland, what else could explain that stumbling somnambulant
walk? She was howling above the music for Elizabeth had not yet
seen her. She was screaming and howling: she was shrieking. And
then Elizabeth turned round and the music stopped and he saw with
inevitable finality the women moving towards her across the space
which separated them from her and on which the shadows fell.

And then he himself was walking towards her. She was weeping
and cursing, she was almost falling among the hollows of the field.
The women were converging on her, they made a circle around her
as if to protect her from the consequences of her own cries. And then
he himself was there, he was in the sacred ring of pity and help, he
was holding out his hands for the telegram, he was reading it, he was
putting his hands on hers, he was saying, "We must take you home."
He was walking towards the car and his wife was by his side and
Morag Bheag was between them. He knew that every movement he
was making, every word that was said, would be analysed by the
spectators for later conversation, but that did not prevent him from
knowing that out of that gossip and watchfulness there was also
emerging compassion and tears and indeed he noticed that Elizabeth
was openly crying.

He and his wife had reached the car. He opened the door and Morag Bheag entered it. She was sitting beside his wife in the back seat, her face working but her voice silent. In her hand she clutched the crumpled telegram. He found that even as he eased the clutch he could pray. It was as if his whole body were gushing forth grief and happiness like a fruit whose taste was both sharp and sweet on his tongue.

He heard his wife talking to Morag Bheag, "You'll stay with us tonight. It will be all right. We'll look after you." The car moved forward from the field on to the road. The village would be forgotten for a while. We are free, he thought, God made us free. It is natural that if there is freedom there should be pain. Endless joy would be impossible for man, could not be sustained. He saw ahead of him as he drove the two lovers returning from the wood, the girl clutching a radio in her hand.

In the back Morag Bheag was whimpering like a beaten dog. Invisible blows rained on her continually from the sky. The picture of her son sprang up in front of her eyes, absolutely mercilessly. His face was round and red cheeked, his hair was long, and he didn't wear a tie. He was sitting at the back of the Sunday class looking loutish and impudent. He was talking to another boy who was sitting beside him. Now and again his eyes would meet the minister's with a defiant stare and then would slowly drop.

"Sh, sh," said his wife over and over again as if she were calming a child. The car drove through the deserted village and turned up towards the manse. To the right of him he could see the bramble berries like drops of blood on their tree.

He opened the car door and both of them helped Morag Bheag into the house. "I will make some tea," his wife said in a whisper. He and Morag Bheag were together. He said in a strong voice, "There is no sadness such as you are suffering. But faith will make us whole. Faith will really make us whole. God Himself lost His only son."

We are free, he thought, we are really free to live and to die. If it were not so we would have been told. Don't look for the kingdom of God elsewhere. The kingdom of God is all round you. Even in the eyes of this grieving woman, even in her helpless curses, the chain stretches to infinity.

"Let us pray," he said and even as he knelt and prayed he saw the

Spanish doll veiled in a black net, skirted in a scalloped pink, toe pointed and alert, a waterfall of hair streaming down her back.

"We are free," he said, "we are each in the care of the other."